BELOW
LEVEL 7

DAVID ORANGE

World Castle Publishing, LLC
Pensacola, Florida
Copyright © 2024 David Orange
Hardback ISBN: 9798341226517
Paperback ISBN: 9798891262904
eBook ISBN: 9798891262911
First Edition World Castle Publishing, LLC, November 5, 2024
http://www.worldcastlepublishing.com
Licensing Notes
Cover: Cover Designs by Karen
Cover-designs-by-karen.com
Editor: Karen Fuller

ACKNOWLEDGEMENT

I want to thank veteran Broadway theatre and film actor Joel Leffert, who co-wrote the completed screenplay for Below Level 7 with me.

PREFACE

Below Level 7 isn't a story for the faint of heart. Some will find it challenging and unpalatable to digest. Although comprised of fictional characters but based on real-life ones, a growing number of people across America believe the setting to be science fact, even though its subject matter is a source of speculation, conjecture, and even tremendous ridicule. This harrowing, highly documented novel will challenge peoples' parameters of reality, suggesting that all is not what it seems regarding how our world runs. How you view Below Level 7 may shock you into opening your once closed mind. Anything and everything is a possibility. Ultimately, it is up to you to decide what truth you wish to believe. If all or most of this story proves entirely accurate, may your conscience guide you?

CHAPTER 1

Sam Dawson drove his Jeep Wrangler Willy wagon through the rugged countryside of the Jicarilla Apache Reservation, filled with mountains, mesas, and sagebrush flats as tumbleweeds rolled by amidst the wind-swirling dust. This beautiful southern Rocky Mountain scenery also had streams, lakes, and high semi-desert land, great for fishing and hunting. The area stuck in the mind of this tightly wound ex-soldier after being at war with Apache Harry Hickey and hearing how his Jicarilla Indian Reservation was known for having the top Big Bull Elk hunting in America. The tribe maintained Horse Lake Mesa Game Park, the largest single elk enclosure in the country at 14,500 acres. For some reason, he never made it hunting here, feeling his home state of Colorado had plenty of wilderness in their great outdoors to satisfy him. But not to end his life. He would do that here, over the border.

He passed a road sign: "Welcome to New Mexico — the Land of Enchantment." Minutes later, he rode by another: "Jicarilla Indian Reservation."

"Hick-a-ree-ya," Sam pronounced phonetically. "Well, Harry, wherever you are, I made it the place you always jawed about in our Afghan days."

In this far northern New Mexico area, he stopped at a fishing and hunting store where the window sign proclaimed: September Bow Hunting Season Licenses."

Sam paid the steep price for a week's hunting license inside the store and picked up various other supplies. He drove along a dirt forest ranger road that cut through a forest, blanketing the area. Sam owned several vehicles but wanted to use the original go-anywhere, a do-anything Wrangler Willy Wagon for his final trip as a Special Forces military man to the core, even though he became forced to retire. It became known by its nickname, "Jeep," made famous during WWII and used heavily by every military division and much of the Allied Forces.

Fifteen minutes later, he was at a lone cabin in the thick Ponderosa pines: firewood stacked nearby, outhouse, cooking pit, but little else except for wildlife sounds. The cabin's insides were ultra Spartan--one bunk bed, sink, fire stove, oil lantern, and no electricity.

Sam looked about at its scarceness. "Well, the ad said no frills."

Later in the evening, after finishing a fish meal, he emptied a bottle of Jack Daniels. The whiskey had become his best friend after his war days ended — his foxhole buddy. Like many soldiers, he was drowning his life in the amber fluid. He didn't want to die, but the truth was that he had nothing to live for.

Sam's patched-up heart no longer worked; his wife had found someone else, and their daughter was grown. From his breast pocket, he removed a folded magazine page of his ex, Karen — striking looking with long blond hair and curves in all the right places. She flashed a brilliant smile in an advertisement for toothpaste. A man's arm was wrapped around her waist, going for a kiss. Sam enlarged one image of them kissing.

"Well, Jack," Sam said to the bottle, "my career's over, marriage dead, a life unable to deal with anymore."

He took his .357 Magnum double-action revolver and cocked it under his chin. "If I'm history to the Special Forces and my wife, tomorrow after I bag a Bighorn Elk and call my little girl one last time, it's check-out time for this has-been."

In the morning, Sam awakened huddled in blankets with a mother of a headache, the fire stove only embers. He left the bed to make coffee before adjusting the portable solar charger to power his cell phone. He reached for a vial of pills. The label read: Silicon Dioxide. Sam took out two pills containing flint traces in their composition and gulped them down.

"You're so full of shit," he said to himself. "No wonder you're constipated."

Several cups of strong black coffee helped clear his head enough to drive into the harsh mountain landscape, kicking up sand and dirt. He went to a whole Ponderosa and Pinion pine forest area in mountainous terrain, inundated mesas, and sagebrush flats and parked his ride concealed in the woodlands. The reservation habitat had nearly 850,000 acres of lakes, buttes, Ponderosa pine forests, and pinion juniper mesas. Sam stepped out into the scenic and tranquil setting as the omnipresent low wind bit into him. He eventually entered the 14,500-acre Horse Lake Mesa, managed exclusively for trophy bull elk.

It was only a short time until he spotted a Big Horned Elk and took his hunting bow and arrow to take it down. It was a huge bull, around seven hundred pounds, light tan, legs and neck darker than the body, long antlers, perhaps weighing forty-five pounds. Sam knew when alarmed, Bull elks raised their heads high, opened their eyes wide, tipped up their nose, and tilted their antlers back. This Bull, however, did none of that, staring at Sam and letting out bellows, unafraid.

He saw the beast dead, but his hands trembled so much that he lowered the bow. Trying again produced the same results. "Some war hero I am," he said in a slur. "A loser up until the end."

He took a swig of amber from his flask and stared at his hands, which were marked with scars from years of combat, the skin rough, and the high desert cold already working on splitting and cracking his fingertips. The Big Horn gave one last gaze at him, unafraid, gave a bugling, bellowing squeal whistle ending with a grunt before moving on.

Sam had another opportunity to bag a buck but failed again to execute. Disgusted with himself and hungry, he headed for the lake to catch his dinner. The ex-soldier wanted to tell himself it wasn't a clear shot but knew it was a lie. He couldn't kill the giant beast and asked himself *what was happening. Am I checking out of this life as a wimp?*

Disgusted with himself, he headed for a lake near fourteen miles of Navajo River to try his luck fishing.

Returning to the cottage several hours later, Sam cooked a bass meal while swigging whiskey again as if it were water. The amber warmed him in the frosty night air that had a real bite. Afterward, he continued drinking his way into yet another stupor. When the bottle was empty, he grabbed his Magnum, checking the firearm's chamber to see it loaded. No one had to tell him that it produced so much recoil and muzzle that it was generally considered unstable for use as a police weapon. A magnum round contained more explosives than any other cartridges of the same size. Also, its rapid-fire was difficult and strenuous on the users' hands, but all Sam had to do was get off one precise shot.

The bottle drained, and he checked his Magnum's chamber before tossing it into the air and firing at it. Not even close.

The Magnum lay by his side, sending a silent message, a promise to end his pain, tormenting him. Sam shivered from the snapping cold piercing through his cotton clothing.

I should have brought my Irish wool sweater, but then he laughed. It didn't matter what the nighttime temperature was. Self-pity overpowered him about his life or the one he would soon cease to have. He felt remorseful about his daughter Carla; what would she think of him as a coward? *She'll get over it,* he convinced himself. *Women always do. They're more resilient.* Before reaching this moment at the end of his life, he'd read that while a parent's suicide would never stop being an important event in their lives, with the help, they could recover their emotional health and vitality.

Sam struggled to erase other ghastly images of his wife with other men. While he'd been fighting for his country, she'd been screwing like an alley cat. Karen kept telling him that she was lonely and that while she married him, he married the military. Sam couldn't lie to himself; that was true. The stress at home reared an angry head. The war in the Middle East had become Vietnam on steroids. He'd be over there for eight or nine months and then rotate back home only to have to go back again.

Word got out among his troops about his wife's infidelity; some soldiers offered a silent expression of condolence. As humans often did, others enjoyed his misfortune, glad it wasn't them. Marriage breakups among enlisted men increased due to soldiers re-enlisting, unable to let go. Sam lost faith in people and their promises, and since he was too busy fighting wars, the slut ex-wife got custody of their daughter and a big part of his paycheck.

If that wasn't enough, his heroic exploits during missions were, for the most part, unknown to the public. He was a quiet soldier defending his country, upholding its Constitution, and getting fucked up.

"I traveled a long way along some roads not paved!" he said, amused, picking up the weapon to feel the cold round barrel he pressed against his cheek. "I can't take the bumps anymore. Nor the ticking bombs in my head waiting to go off." He gazed fondly at his gun. "Most don't understand what I feel, but you do."

The military prepared him to kill in war, but no one told him how to reverse the process to allow him to decompress and assimilate into society. He became just another unfortunate, unable to acclimate to new pressures and environments upon returning from combat.

Sam re-positioned the Magnum barrel under his chin. "Goodbye, cruel world."

Leonard Cohen's *Halleluiah* broke the silence. He sadly smiled when noting the I.D. caller. His daughter had set up the song on his cell, knowing how much he liked it. Now wasn't the time to talk to her. The music stopped suddenly, echoing a silence like the one he felt in his heart. The night became quiet again; only the sparks from the grill cooking the shriveled fish seemed alive. Leonard Cohen was back, and although the song was his favorite, it made him feel very lonely this time.

Flipping a contemplative coin in his mind, he answered. "Checking up on the old man?" he asked, concentrating on hiding his drinking.

"Someone has to." It was a young woman's voice, his only offspring, Carla.

"Miss me yelling at you?"

"Hardly. Mom does enough of that."

"Listen, Carla," Sam said, "I was going to call to tell you never in my life did I ever love someone as I did you."

"Did? So you're done loving me? Finished like another whiskey bottle?"

"Hey. If stores gave deposits on empties, you'd go to Harvard now. How's your mom and the new guy?"

"A freeloader allergic to work," Carla answered without hesitation. "So stupid for her to divorce you. And I need a break from those two necking like teens. Er, sorry."

"Don't be. Mom got tired of my vacant space in the bed."

"And I hate her for that," Carla said with bitterness. "Listen, my vacation plans fell through."

"No, Cancun? What about your—"

"We broke up," Carla said glumly.

"Sorry to hear. Must run in the family."

"I need to get away. Was hoping I could visit you."

Sam set the Magnum on his lap. "Uh, not a good idea."

"Why not if you love me so much?"

"To do what? Watch me drink? It's a two-hour-a-half drive."

"Please. I need you. Just for a couple of days."

Sam tried to talk her out of it. "Uh, there's no electricity, no T.V."

"I can deal. I need the time to work on a term paper. Promise I won't be in the way." Silence on the other end. "I need you, Daddy. You got an extra bunk?"

He sighed, looked at his revolver, and set it aside. "I'll sleep on the floor, softer than the mattress."

"Then I'll see you tomorrow early evening."

"All right, but promise to get here before sunset."

"Promise."

Sam gave directions, and the call ended. He picked up his Magnum again and sank to the cold ground with a bitter laugh. Wiping emotion from his eyes and drinking the last of the whiskey, he rehashed an episode of his life that immensely helped him to slide into the abyss.

———————

Three Years Ago,

The Middle East

At a fortified desert compound, a Black Hawk helicopter with radar-evading modifications and flying without lights on a moonless evening appeared out of nowhere to hover just outside the guarded complex. Rappelling down were U.S. Special Operations Forces operatives wearing night vision goggles.

Leading the assault group dedicated explicitly to high-risk counterterrorism operations was Sergeant Sam Dawson. A laser-focused, tightly wound man, both body and mind, with lightning-quick reflexes and power, had kept him alive through heavy combat action. He advanced with several soldiers trained to endure anxiety-filled operations.

Among them was lean and chiseled-faced Private Harry "Hatchet" Chama, an American Indian from a tribe near Dulce, New Mexico. Alongside him was Private Brock Garcia, a mixed-black Latino with a crew cut, thick muscles, and wild eyes, the kind of guy you'd want on your side in a fight.

They used small crossbows with infrared sighting as primary weapons to combat the enemy — one hundred percent quiet. Prepared for everything, several compound sentries were taken out with deadly bow accuracy before they could fire a shot. Sam and his men planted plastic explosives on their way to a sealed-off room. In Sam's pocket were photographs and a physical description of the suspect person inside. This soldier also wore a noise-canceling headset, blocking nearly everything besides his heartbeat.

Sam and his team breached the compound, blowing open the door, ready to handle a firefight to take out their "target." However, all those inside were sleeping women and children. They moved to the second and third floors, but no one was there except for an older couple rousted from their sleep. The women were screaming in Arabic as they ripped off their veils for signs of trickery that weren't there.

"Negative! Negative!" Sam said over communication.

And he heard: "Abort! Cover your tracks!"

"Roger." Sam relayed to his men: "Abort! Fuckin' abort! Shit!"

The Special Forces team hastily retreated and raced outside to their hovering copter. Sentry gunfire surprised them. Some of his men took out Heckler & Koch MP7-s tucked into the small of their backs.

Sam ordered the team to board the whirlybird while, completely disregarding his safety, rushing back to his fallen brother. "You're not fuckin' getting greased here. You're comin' with us, Hatchet! Those kids need you on the Res. Let's haul ass—"

The offensive soldier team hastily retreated to the waiting copter but was caught in a line of fire coming from an adjacent building. Bullets ripped into Private Hatchet Chama's hip; he lost control of his leg, crumbling to the ground. Seeing Chama dragging himself slowly along, Sam grabbed him, tossing him over his shoulder. Just then, Sam felt an impact in the chest. The frontal area of the bullet's pointy tip, so small, wasn't caught by the fibers, allowing it to pierce through his flak jacket vest deep into the trauma plate. The impact sent Sam reeling back before he dropped to a knee.

If this is the end, so be it, Sam thought. He knew the rules of the game. Some who go to war never return. Staying calm under the immense pressure, through sheer grit, he managed again to lift Hatchet Chama onto his shoulders. Staggering to the chopper and dragged into it, the whirly soared into the night sky through a barrage of fire.

Enemy Sentries advanced on Sam. A standoff ensued

as they and Special Forces aimed weapons at each other.

In deep pain, Sam took a hand-held device from his flak jacket and shouted in Arabic. "We planted explosives," he called. "I press this, and the women and children inside instantly visit Allah!"

He staggered closer to them, ready to press the detonation device. The sentries looked at one another bewildered, some backing off, except the head one.

"We hide no one, but you attack us... Murderers!" he said in defiance." The standoff continued as he pleaded, "I...I have a daughter inside. She's my life!"

Sam looked up into the night sky. "What happens after what I'm about to do is up to your Allah. Let his decision rest on his head."

Sam shocked both sides by setting the bombing device on the ground. As he staggered towards the waiting chopper, the head Sentry signaled his men not to fire and carefully picked up the device. The helicopter, with Sam aboard, ascended into the night sky.

Sam was flown out of the country to Balad, Iraq, to the U.S. military's largest hospital. Within minutes, a medical team inserted an implantable cardioverter defibrillator into Sam's chest. They put him into cardiac arrest to use the defibrillator to shock him to a normal rhythm. Later, they installed a biventricular device, placing leads into the left side of his heart through the vein.

Convalescing, he became visited by Major Jason Briggs, a white-haired, husky-faced commander, thick-necked, with brass dripping from his uniform.

"I don't know how you're alive, soldier," Briggs said. "That bullet must've bounced off your heart."

"Yeah. The whole damn raid gave me heartburn, sir. What happened? Intel got it wrong?"

"They think we just missed him. The fog of war. The end of the war for you."

"So just like that, I'm history?" Sam asked.

"In the field, yes. But we still need you."

"Shuffling papers behind a desk? With all due respect, fuck that, sir!"

"Did I say shuffling papers?" Briggs asked. "Our Top Secret projects are into some very complex and interesting military projects, especially 'thinking underground.' I could introduce you to some people."

"Sir, all I know is boots on the ground."

"Take your time." Major Briggs stopped short. "Let your family know what you look like."

Sam looked out the window.

"Sorry, Sam," Briggs continued. "You deserve the Medal of Honor, but this mission never happened."

"I figured as much. No harm done. How's Hatchet?"

"A shattered hip. The Injun will limp but live. I owe you, soldier. We all do."

Briggs saluted him and left.

Sam gazed with a scowl at his reflection on the window pane. He wondered if anyone in the real world would understand his folly of war journey to feed his habit. Just as morphine was a potent painkiller that often becomes highly addictive, the war game was Sam's drug, a powerful and almost lethal addiction. He knew nothing in the outside world would cure his craving for the danger in battle. Dependency didn't work cold turkey. Combat was a part of him, like blood in his veins. With his days of being in the thick of a kill zone over, that depressing thought made his mind feel like it was starting to pull off its girders. The thrill of combat had twisted his mind, slicing and dicing it into little pieces and spitting it out. His heart, which gave its all to protect America, had been tossed into the scrap heap.

CHAPTER 2

Present Day
The Following Afternoon

Carla Dawson, energetic and cute with an easy dimpled smile, drove her Jeep the following afternoon following GPS directions. She passed a road sign: "Leaving Colorado." Shortly after that, another reading, "Dulce, New Mexico — 5 miles."

Her cell rang. "Your nose is still like a bloodhound's," she told her dad. "I'm only five miles away."

"Always sense your presence."

"Hmmm."

"It's getting dark. You'll miss my cottage among the thick pines. Pull into Dulce's main street and the Gulf gas Station at the only red light in town. I'll be there in fifteen minutes. Mark it."

"It's marked."

Minutes later, Carla, headlights on, passed a sign reading:

Dulce, New Mexico
Pop. 2,755
Jicarilla Apache Indian Reservation

She answered her cell. "Your nose is still keen. I'm—

"I'm in town," Sam's voice said. "Always sense your presence."

"Hmm. I'll see you in a couple of minutes."

Carla set aside her cell, suddenly swerving to avoid hitting a jackrabbit, the quick move causing her to slide off the road.

"Damn, scared the hell out of me!" she said to herself. "At least I didn't hit it."

Suddenly, something swooped above the top of the car, shaking it sideways before a pattering of footsteps. Carla became spooked. "What the hell?"

Carla turned the ignition key, the motor grinding until it turned over.

With a touch of the gas pedal, the jerk caused whatever was on the roof to slide, a sickle claw appearing at the top of the window before it pushed off. Silence. Carla was back on the road driving off, the pedal to the metal.

Sam was at the town gas station; Carla jumped out of her car, rushing to hug her father.

Carla was on edge. "Something just happened!"

She began describing. Finally, " — Dad, it shook the car! It sprang off the windshield, *whoosh*, then disappeared! Too dark to know what it was."

Sam went to her car, pointing to several claw scratches on the windshield. "Maybe a mountain lion, which is aplenty here on the Res."

"Dad, it shook the car. It was dark, but I think I saw a clawed foot like some raptor out of Jurassic Park before it leaped into the darkness."

Sam's instincts went into battle mode, looking for an elusive enemy to find before it found them. He looked about for shadows and movement but saw nothing but silence. Before making this trip, he'd done his homework, aware of New Mexico's healthy population of mountain lions and black bears; thus, hunters must learn to take precautions and avoid dangerous encounters. He'd read of a recent meeting of a man who liked to bathe and shave on a rock ledge about sixty yards from his home. The state Department of Game and Fish determined the lion attacked him just below the ridge, dragged his body a short distance, and then ate and buried parts of it.

Sam looked around the sparse, mainly wasteland area. "Whatever it was is gone. I'll sweep the area tomorrow."

When they drove their vehicles up the windy, rugged terrain to his cottage, Sam helped with her meager baggage brought inside.

"This is it?" she asked, underwhelmed as she set her rucksack on the floor.

"Told you it was small. You can sleep and leave tomorrow. I understand."

"No, no, it's okay; it's just that I've never seen anything this tiny. Like it's for the Hobbits!"

Sam got the fire stove going and asked. "This term paper...what's it about?"

"Creative writing class. Anything I want as long as it's original."

"You could write about the original owners here—the Apaches. You're about to live like they once did."

"Not bad. By the way, I'm starving. I could eat a horse."

"Well, an old friend once told me animal hunting was good up here, but so far, fish will have to do."

Soon, Sam was serving the catch he caught from the outdoor grill, stopping to gulp some whiskey.

"I could help at the shop during the summer."

"What do you know about cars?"

"I could do the bookkeeping."

"That'd be nice, except it's too far to travel."

"Not if I lived with you..."

Sam raised his brows and gave her a big hug. "What about Mom?"

"I'm half yours; she'll just have to understand."

That touched Sam more than Carla would ever know; he hugged her.

Sam thought again of being away to war, re-upping repeatedly, which led to his divorce. He admitted to himself, his wife, and a psychiatrist that getting into firefights brought him a tremendous "rush." Now, in civilian life, he realized how many people became hooked on drugs, heroin, and cocaine. But for Sam, the best, most pleasurable high he could ever get was a natural adrenaline rush—somebody trying to kill him. There became nothing that would ever come to that rush.

Behind a thick pine tree came a slight rustle of bushes and heavy breathing, studying the fire stove-lit lodge. The creature leaned a razor-sharp sickle claw against the tree, bark falling from the trunk. Its silhouette retreated into darkness, footsteps crunching on the pine needles.

Early in the morning, Carla was bundled in blankets in the bunk while Sam added logs to the fire.

"Mornin'," he said. "I came up with the first line to your story. 'As I stumbled out of our winter lodge into the cold air to relieve myself, I remembered a strange dream I had about indoor plumbing.'"

Carla rolled her eyes, yawned, and returned under the covers' warmth. "Which reminds me, I hope you're taking the constipation pills I sent you?"

"Yep. Call me Mister Regular." He took out the vial from his pocket and popped one.

"Good," she said with a giggle. "Don't want you in a

crappy mood while I'm here."

Soon, Sam was packed up and ready to try again for an elk, but if he waffled, then fishing. "Again, don't go wandering off. There are lots of black bears and mountain lions in these parts. Do your writing until I get back late afternoon."

Carla used a little girl's voice. "Yes, Daddy."

"Your cell's charged up, so so we can commo throughout the day."

Carla mock saluted her military-bent dad. "Yes, sir. I got it, sir. Watch out for Big Foot, sir."

Sam gave her a peck on the cheek before leaving to drive off.

Eventually, Carla awakened fully, set up her makeshift desk, and got to work on her writing project. By afternoon, she was writing feverishly when her cell rang. "Everything's fine, Dad. And you?"

"How about a fresh, juicy trout dinner tonight?"

"Sounds great."

Later in the day, towards dusk, inside the cabin, Sam's only child rummaged through her bag for a box of sanitary napkins, but it was empty. "Damn, what did the Indian gals do?"

Carla drove towards Dulce, headlights on and music blasting from the radio. Just before she left the pine tree track for a paved road, her motor suddenly died, as did the radio and the running lights.

"What now...?"

She glided the car beside a thicket of pines and tried to start it again, but it wouldn't turn over. No lights, no power. She got out, trying to figure out what the problem was. She tried calling her dad, but her cell went dead.

Reaching inside the open door for her cell, Carla was distracted by a lone light beam descending, freezing her helplessly in her tracks as she became seemingly hypnotized. A hazy orange beam fell from above, freezing her in her tracks. *What the hell?* She had never seen anything like it; the beam shimmered with hues of yellow and gold. Carla was mesmerized by the beautiful effect. A prickly sensation passed through the upper half of her body, paralyzing her.

She screamed, but the sound seemed to bounce back at her. Her heart pounded, ready to break out of her chest as she slowly started to lift off the ground! She tried to move away from the beam but couldn't; it was as if somebody had poured thick molasses over her.

Suddenly, her feet began leaving the ground! Through the eyes of an intruder seemingly more comfortable in shadows, it moved closer as it slid silently through the trees before suddenly rising above them.

When the intruder was gone, the car lights went back on; the radio music started playing as two eagle feathers floated to the ground alongside the car.

––––––––

Sam began packing his outdoor gear by the lake and looked at his watch before making a call. "Carla? Pick up. Call me. Four o'clock. On my way to the cabin."

About to leave in his van, Sam again dialed, having to leave another message. "If you're gabbing with one of your friends, Carla, hang up and call me ASAP."

He tore off in his ride. Sam didn't notice his daughter's car as he raced up the dirt and gravel road to the cabin. He rushed inside, didn't see her, and checked the outhouse. His trained eyes studied the ground for additional clues—nothing. He shouted into the darkness, "Carla! Carla!"

It was twilight as he drove back down the road slowly until he saw Carla's car parked under the pines, the car lights and radio still on. He looked inside and saw her phone on the seat. Footprints were by the car's side but nowhere else. Then he noticed the two eagle feathers by the door, dark gray with a small whitish patch at the base, like those of a bald eagle. He stalked the nearby countryside, searching for his daughter. War experience taught him that fear would provide nothing but cost him a lot. He might never overcome it one hundred percent, but he could manage and control it. But damn, this was his *daughter!* He checked her cell, but it was dead.

Seeing absolutely nothing, Sam rushed to his car and peeled out towards Dulce. He stopped by the Police Station and saw a sign on the door with a number to call the Sheriff. "Fuckin' hick town."

He dialed his cell. Twenty minutes later, a State Police car pulled up, and the beefy Sheriff Wilson came out, whose posture seemed to show that he was proud of his girth. "Sorry about that. Damn, flu season has two sheriffs out sick. Is there a problem?"

"My daughter went missing on this reservation!"

The last traces of sunset could faintly be seen over the distant mountains as Sam told what happened, showing the Indian feathers.

"Hope they're not at it again," the Sheriff said.

"Who?"

"The Jicarilla Indians on the Res or another tribe nearby."

"You think so?"

"Ain't much of anyone else 'round here."

"We're wasting time. Get me to these Indians."

"Hold on; no proof of that yet," Sheriff said. "Most people missin' on the Res get lost in the deep caves and can't find their way back out. More caves in this state than any other in America."

Sam was becoming irritated. "Carla would never go in

alone."

"That's what all parents say."

That riled Sam, who got into the guy's face. "Listen, you! I have friends in higher places than the President. Get some fucking help NOW, or I'll make some calls!"

"Okay, calm down," Sheriff Carl squeamishly answered when seeing Sam's wild-eyed expression. "I'll get a search party going."

Sam fired rapid instructions. "Also, contact the NCIC — get Carla's profile into the database, and match it to other Missing Persons nationwide. And check NAMUS."

"NAMUS, what the hell—"

"National Missing and Unidentified Persons System."

Sheriff Wilson swallowed bile, unhappy about Sam's orders, but he didn't know yet who this guy was. Before Wilson checked anything on his daughter, he'd search for Sam Dawson.

Law enforcement cars and dune buggies parked near police tape cordoned off the area of Carla's car. Police, local volunteers, bloodhound dogs, and search dune buggies went off to explore the rugged desert mountain ground.

"Weird," Sam said to Sheriff Wilson. "No footprints once she got out of the car. As if she was lifted, Eagle feathers, but even a large eagle can't carry an adult off the ground."

"Don't think so."

"And not a helicopter 'cause there's no disruption of ground soil from the rotor's downwash."

"Don't know about that stuff."

Sam drifted off to make a call. "Karen...sorry to say this, but Carla's missing."

"What? In New Mexico? In the goddamn middle of nowhere?"

"Yeah. Yeah. Carla left the cottage on her own. We

found the car but not her. But we will. The police are searching now."

"What the hell good are you! That's my daughter!"

"*Our* daughter."

"This is all because of you!"

"How can you say that?"

"Carla canceled her trip to be with you, worried about your depression and heavy drinking!"

"She said she broke up with her boyfriend. Oh shit."

"Oh, shit, that sums you up. She's worried about you becoming major suicidal at the breaking point."

"Dammit," Sam moaned. "Look, Missing Person organizations have already been notified. Contact her friends. Maybe she told someone more than we know. Contact that Social Network stuff that she's wired. Put up photos of Carla everywhere. I'll do the same here—"

"I can't believe you allowed her—"

"I'm not in the mood for bashing now! Bye."

"I'm coming down there!"

"No, I need you to stay put and do a lot of Intel for me. Later."

Sam cut her off and drove on. Carla knew he'd hit rock bottom, even though he tried to hide it, always pumping himself up around her, putting on a cheery face. He guessed his daughter had her old man's instincts and could see through camouflage and bullshit.

Sam went back to the Sheriff. "Where do you start first?"

"We'll search the immediate perimeter some more, but the organized hunt won't begin 'til sunrise."

"Whatever," Sam answered in a mumble. "I'll continue solo."

"Mr. Dawson," Sheriff shot back, "don't go MIA out

there! The Res is damn near twenty by thirty miles! Wild animals up the wazoo! Hey! Do you hear me?"

Sam shot him a stern look. "My daughter's life is at stake. Until authorities find a lead, I'll take matters into my own hands."

The Sheriff mumbled under his breath, "Asshole."

Sam hopped into his station wagon and tore off, panic rising.

The Sheriff didn't like this renegade type of guy at all.

After a very short distance, Sam slammed on the brakes, his chest hitting the stirring wheel. He took a deep breath and exhaled slowly, trying to relieve the pressure building in him. He thought, *Come on, Sergeant Dawson, get your shit together. This mission I'm about to go on is the most important I've ever had.* He stepped on the gas, taking off towards the mountains.

Suicide became the furthest thing in his mind. In a matter of minutes, everything had changed; that's the way his shitty life worked. His great fear now was never seeing Carla again. Suddenly, he had a reason for living. *I'm lost and in a terrible place.*

He stopped near one of the caves, an area so quiet he thought he could hear himself think, the silence as familiar as his skin. *Who would take Carla and why?* He'd experienced that fear many times during missions, and it invariably preceded danger. However, he always knew his enemy in the war, but now he had no clue about this one.

A grim Sam, knife at his belt, Tactical LED flashlight in hand, and a Magnum Colt stuck in the small of his back, he continued searching until he observed a camping party in the woods.

He crawled close to them, but it had nothing to do with Carla. The ex-Special Forces soldier backtracked away. Hours later, he was climbing up to a rocky ledge. There was the glow from a fire near the mouth of a cave. He saw a young woman leaning over with hair like Carla's.

Sam snuck up behind and put the gun to the young man's head in military mode. "Don't move!"

The male youth, in fear, nearly lost his voice. "Please, take our money!"

Realizing the girl wasn't Carla, Sam lowered his weapon. "Sorry, wrong person. Miss, are you all right?

"She sprained her ankle inside the cave," her male companion answered.

Sam took out a photo of a smiling, wholesome Carla. "Have you seen her?"

"No. Sorry," the young man answered.

"My missing daughter. Call me if you do." Sam handed over a card. "C'mon, I'll give you a ride to town."

CHAPTER 3

There was a hint of dawn in the desert as the sunrise as blue and violet colors began to awaken. Sam sat on a rock, exhausted, lost for the first time. He drove towards town as Wilson's expanded Search Party resumed the hunt.

Sam was exhausted from a sleepless night and leaned on his car drinking from a canteen when a pickup with dented doors and missing paint approached on an unpaved logging road, kicking up dust.

An aged, long-haired American Indian climbed out, his weathered face reflecting the harsh high desert life taking its toll on him. Billy Two Snakes, this humbly radiant Indian wearing an eagle-feathered cowboy hat, became trailed by a German shepherd wearing a colored handkerchief around its neck. The elder tried closing the door several times until a few kicks did the trick.

He was from a neighboring Indian band called the Himmarshee, only a mile from the Jicarilla Reservation border. He spoke in the Athabasken linguistic dialect that once migrated out of Canada.

Sheriff Wilson, part Indian but not Jicarilla, couldn't understand his tongue when the old one said, "So, you fat, ugly, sheep-turd. I see they're at it again."

Sam approached the Indian, determined to hold the two eagle feathers up to his face. "Hey! Where's my daughter?"

The dog started to bark. Wilson separated the two men and glared at Sam. "Hey, easy, cowboy, you don't run this show!"

Sam was still in the older man's face, showing the Indian feathers. "These were found by her car. Like the ones in your hat. What do you know about it?"

The Indian mumbled something in his Indian dialect with some scant English. "Rock men here to hide secrets."

"Who knows? Ol' Chief Billy Two Snakes could be," Wilson made the cuckoo sign on his forehead.

Sam backed off a step and looked at the Indian. "You speak English?"

Billy Two Snakes gave Wilson a wary smile. "Tell him." He then pointed to a mesa looming nearby. "The Rock... mountain of many secrets."

"Is that where my daughter is?" Sam asked.

Approaching fast was a black Lincoln Town car bearing government G-14 license plates, tinted windows, and a long antenna, pulling alongside Billy's truck. When its door opened, the dashboard console was full of computers, microphones, cameras, gauges, CO2 monitors, switches, and buttons with voice-operated controls.

Two imposing men dressed in dark suits and Ray-ban sunglasses stepped out to speak to Wilson in hushed tones.

Old Billy spoke out of the side of his mouth to Sam. "Archuleta Rock men come here to hide tracks. What secrets here stay secret." He signaled his dog, and they quickly got in his pickup and drove off as the dark suit men glared at him.

"Hey! Wait!" Sam could not stop Indian Billy as Wilson approached to see him studying the dark-suited men wearing shades. "What do they want?"

"Just military boys from the base here," the Sheriff answered. "They said they haven't seen your girl."

"Maybe so, but I want to talk to them."

He headed for their black town car, but it, too, drove off.

"Those aren't any uniforms, I know. What kind of base is it?"

Sheriff's face took on a stoic look. "Some top secret military stuff. That's all I know."

"This is your town, and you don't know?"

Wilson tried a different tact. "Look, Dulce's a sleepy little desert town, just under three thousand people, but we've got more workforce comin'. We'll find her if she's here."

"What's Archuleta? That Indian called it the Rock, the mountain of many secrets. What's that about?"

The Sheriff answered, "Archuleta is nothin' but a mesa, Mr. Dawson. Anything else the Injuns believes is superstition, just superstition. Nature is also sacred to them — rocks, water, sky, animals, wind, and whatnot." He handed over a cell phone. "Your daughter's. The circuit's fried. Nothin' can be retrieved."

Sheriff Wilson, watching Sam's vehicle peeling up dust, got on his cell. "Sam Dawson is gonna be trouble." He listened and then answered, "Got it."

————————

At sunset, the Search Party continued to comb the area by foot with their bloodhounds while cars and dune buggies checked the roads, a helicopter searching from above.

Sam was with a State Officer checking out openings in large boulder formations and scouring the inside of a cave that was a maze of limestone corridors with unique rock formations and swarms of bat colonies flying about.

"They call it Prairie Dog Cave," the officer said, "because it's like a prairie dog lair, surface openings everywhere."

"We'll check 'em all."

And they just about did, going through cave rooms with abundant large calcite, gypsum, and other mineral formations.

The following morning, Sam awakened in the back seat of his car. His deflated expression told the story. He stretched out and saw Indian Billy nearby, leaning on his truck door and looking at him. The old Indian pointed towards Archuleta Peak, "The Rock," before driving off.

Sam drove away from the nearby search team.

Sheriff Wilson, who had been watching, got on communication. "Dawson could bring a shitload of trouble."

The Dulce area had some of the most beautiful, scenic locations in northern New Mexico between Chama and Farmington, just below Pagosa Springs, Colorado. On the outskirts of town, nearly three miles away at the base of Archuleta Mesa, Sam followed a paved government road thirty-six feet wide going into the area. He then diverted to a dirt track, stopping at a barbed wire fence with a bold sign reading: *Military Area: Strictly Off Limits – Use of Deadly Force Authorized.*

Inside the complex, Sam's trained military eye noted several telemetry trailers and a couple of five-sided buildings with domes. He also took in a black van, several big-wheeled, covered vehicles going into and out of the base, and armed guards stationed on all corners of each building. He memorized some details while tabulating the military headquarters slightly under a mile long. He then left before being spotted.

To further access his target perimeter, he drove the circumference of the Archuleta Mesa, beginning from County Road 357, going north to Lumberton towards the eastern slope and entering the Colorado border, continuing west, then north all the way around. He finally reached the southern hills of the mesa along the Navajo River. It took him about forty-five miles to bring the entire trip, showing the size of the whole Archuleta Mesa area. He had to find out what kind of base that was and why old Indian Billy pointed to it, something Sam sensed the Sheriff wouldn't be much help.

He drove past tangled brush into the sleepy, dusty tribal headquarters community of Dulce near the reservation's northern end. He approached the hamlet and saw a billboard advertising the Best Western Wild Horse Hotel and Casino. Dulce looked like barren land in the desert—merely a "wide spot" in the road, although it did host the nearby Apache Nugget Casino. Some sixth sense in Sam deduced this area was an open desert far from prying eyes.

The town had a gas station, supermarket, True Value hardware store, two churches, and other businesses. A few people moved about Main Street, including some Indians with eagle feathers in their hats. A dog with heavy dust on its coat napped in the sun alongside the roadside.

Sam parked and entered the coffee shop, handed a Missing Person photo of Carla to a server, and explained some particulars. He noticed several patrons eyeing him, speaking to one another in hushed tones.

"My daughter went missing around here yesterday," he announced loudly. "If anyone has any information on where she might be, notify the police or my cell number below the photo. There's a reward. Thanks."

No one reacted beyond looking down in silence, returning to their meals.

"What's wrong with them?" Sam asked the waitress.

"People around here mind their own business. No one wants trouble."

"Trouble from whom?"

The waitress didn't respond; she thumb-tacked the photo alongside several other Missing teen children on the wall.

Sam also read on the bulletin board that Dulce was

initially called "Aqua Dulce." Spanish for sweet water because of natural springs that provided good drinking water for the people and their animals.

Sam sized up the customers. Two sets of twin children were wandering about like each was a brother and sister. The four of them wore dark black sunglasses indoors. They looked at Sam, almost animal-like, pulling down their shades slightly to reveal glistening black eyes, their heads cocked inquisitively, almost like curious puppies. They passed Sam on their way out of the restaurant. Once outside, a car with tinted windows stopped in the middle of the road; the two sets of twins got in, and the car drove off.

Sam couldn't help but feel the town had morbid darkness, and the strange aloofness of the residents added to it.

Several young Indian teens sat in a corner, computers in front of them. They appeared normal-looking, without sunglasses, and paid him little attention. There was a sign on the window: Wi-Fi service available.

Sam went to one sitting alone, reached into his pocket, and took out a twenty-dollar bill. "This is yours if I can have ten minutes on your computer."

The kid took the twenty eagerly. "Sure," he said, moving away to a nearby table.

Sam typed in *Dulce, New Mexico.* He was surprised by nearly a hundred articles about the town's military base, far too many for a place so small. The first article was from Wikipedia's free encyclopedia. What read on the screen didn't mince words: *"Dulce Base is an alleged secret extraterrestrial alien underground facility under Archuleta Mesa on the Colorado-New Mexico border near the town of Dulce.*

Another article detailed 1990 of a crew working for a Japanese television program attempting to document the existence of such an alien base at Dulce. Although he was unsuccessful in locating it, the head of the film crew claimed detainment by the police chief while interviewing the citizens on the street about UFOs and cattle mutilations.

Sam's periphery saw the youth looking at his watch, tabulating the time left to their deal.

Sam didn't read the Wikipedia blurb but moved to the following article's title on page one: *The Subterranean Species Killed 60 People in New Mexico.*

He read a minute's worth and now knew why he hardly ever read stuff on the Web — far too much conspiracy theory catering to the gullible or credulous that ate this nonsense up.

"Uh, sir, that's eleven minutes. Need my computer back."

"Sure, kid. Thanks." He reached into his pocket. "Another twenty if you can answer a question or two."

The youth eyed the money. "I'll try." They sat at an empty table.

Several patrons at the counter looked over to Sam and the youth. The young Indian picked up one of the twenties, forcing the kid to give Sam the routine answer.

"For your good, I strongly advise against snooping around or asking questions," the youth answered. "Some say the place hides a deep, dark secret beneath our feet. Digging for it has put people at risk. Hope you find your daughter."

He got up and left, leaving the twenty on the table.

Sam sat there digesting the Dulce information. It all made him so tightly wound with negatives going through his mind that he now used a technique in the war for mental health. The ex-soldier put his thoughts in a visual self-relaxation, imagining it with every sense of his body — colors, shapes, textures, sounds, smells, temperature, and touch. After going through it several times and the knots easing their grip on Sam, he left the diner, determined to tear this town apart piece by piece until he located his daughter. Carla was out there somewhere on this mission to bring her home. It wasn't the responsibility of the Sheriff and his search team, who would help out for a while and wouldn't finish it — it was his job.

Sam left. Outside, a man was having trouble starting his engine, which coughed and ground. A good ol' boy with substantial red around his neck was at the wheel, trying to get it going.

"I'm a gear monkey handy with cars. Want help?" Sam offered.

"Thanks."

Sam lifted the hood to jiggle some wires. "Try again."

When the grinding sound continued, he took out his utility knife, adjusted it, and the engine turned over. "Loose wire on your fuel injection."

"I owe you a beer."

"Got some time now..."

The guy pointed to the only bar on the street. "Let's down a quick cold one."

Another dark government Lincoln Town car cruising by, parked near the bar. Inside it, different from before, two Archuleta security men observed Sam entering the bar with Roger. These shadowing men guarding the Rock had small glass vials filled with a red solution, the color and the texture of "blood." They sipped from them; a euphoric effect appeared to overtake them.

In an anonymous room, shadowy figures simultaneously "saw and heard" Sam through the eyes and ears of the Rock security men. They weren't looking at any screen. The effect was as if the image was playing out in their minds as they continued to observe the bar.

Sam saddled inside the bar with the man who said, "I'm Roger."

"Sam."

"You from 'round here?"

"Just north of Denver. I came here for trophy hunting."

"You hit Paradise for the big game — especially trophy Big Horn Elk. What rifle are you packin'? I use a .270 or .308 caliber bolt action, a 4 x 14 power scope."

"A bow works just fine."

"An eagle eye, are ya?"

Sam shrugged. "What's up with this town? It's like the Twilight Zone at sunset. Everything's closed, streets empty."

Roger sipped on his suds. "What do you expect from a hole-in-the-wall on the edge of the Res? One motel, gas station, and bar ain't exactly Vegas."

"What are you doing here then?"

"This where I work."

"Doing what, may I ask?"

"A security guard at the base."

"And what's with Archuleta Mesa? I've heard things."

Roger measured his response. "Nothin's true. Dulce jus' has a strange vibe made into a story created to try and make this place into another Roswell, that's all. Not a house of horrors or whatever they think the mesa is."

"I heard Archuleta Mesa called the Rock, the mountain of secrets." Sam hedged. "Can you explain that?"

In that anonymous room, the shadowy figures monitored what Roger saw and heard.

Roger downed the remainder of his beer. "Mountain of secrets? Don't know nothin' about that, but it's no secret I gotta shove off to work."

"Thanks for the suds."

"Are you camping out or getting a roof over your

head?"

"I'm staying at a cabin in the middle of nowhere, but I might get a place near town. Why?"

"I flop just outside town at the Gilmore Apartments," Roger informed. "No frills but clean, cheap. They got vacancies."

"I'll check it out. Thanks."

Sam watched him leave from the window, only to notice the dark Lincoln Town sedan idling across the street. The tinted windows kept him from seeing who was inside and why he'd caught someone's interest. Sam again couldn't shake the sense of an air of evil hanging like a blanket over Dulce. He couldn't see it, but he could feel it, just like in combat, the calm before the storm of a firefight erupting out of nowhere.

CHAPTER 4

On a lonely road facing barren wasteland and mesas, Sheriff Wilson's patrol car maneuvered to park next to another government sedan with two more Rock security men in suits and Ray-ban sunglasses. These shadowing security men had small glass vials filled with a red solution, the color and the texture of "blood." They sipped from them; a euphoric effect appeared to overtake them.

"What else you got?" Wilson asked.

"Dawson was a decorated Special Forces soldier, now retired," said the Rock security man driving the government car. "They want a short leash on him."

"A chokehold sounds good."

The Rock Men drive off.

Wilson opened his glove compartment to clutch a vial with the same red solution as the Rock Men drank. Sipping it also gave him seemingly an instant euphoria.

Sam was inside an Outdoorsman Store at the edge of town inspecting high-powered rifles, pistols, and bows with crosshair sights. After purchasing what he needed, he asked the senior man behind the counter, "Do people often go missing around here?"

The older man considered the question. "I guess they go missing as much as they do anywhere else. Most get found, and some do not. Why are you asking?"

"No reason." As Sam left the store, his peripheral vision detected the storekeeper observing him suspiciously from the window.

Sam drove past the cordoned-off area where Carla had disappeared. Sam spotted another black Lincoln Town car following. When Carla's father reached a bend in the road, he pulled off quickly, unseen. After the sedan passed, he headed in the opposite direction, passing Archuleta Mountain—the Rock.

Sam drove back to the cordoned-off area marking Carla's disappearance site. As expected, another black Lincoln Town car followed him safely in the distance. After it passed, Sam headed opposite Archuleta Mesa. He pulled off quickly before being seen when he came to a bend in the road.

During his soldier days, he'd become tested after showing a sixth sense on the battlefield. An intuition allowed him to detect patterns amid uncertain scenarios quickly. The findings ended for the military. Regardless, Sam still had that sixth sense, like a dog able to hear frequencies not audible to human ears.

Driving off, Sam again sensed Carla's essence. He'd bet these Rock men, or whatever they were called, knew where. A part of him, the loving father, wanted to go after these men and snap their necks if they withheld information on Carla's whereabouts. But he'd bet a lousy move like that would bring down a whole flock of these birds of prey on him. No, he had to be as careful as a boxer entering the ring against an unknown opponent, feeling him out, flicking a jab here and there before finding a weakness to allow him to deliver the knockout punch.

Dulce Installation Base – Nightmare Hall

Carla became forced to stay awake, fearful of what could happen. She'd seen what looked like human-like creatures in shadows but were simultaneously different. She was hungry, thirsty, and hadn't eaten anything. Was this a hallucination? *Had this situation she was in been going on for two days*? Again, Carla detected the strong smell of formaldehyde. It had her recalling being in biology class and the professor dissecting frogs and worms preserved in the stuff. There also was the stench of blood, perhaps dry blood that smelled mustier, more rotten than wet. Carla suspected she was underground in some complex, maybe a big cave. She saw different corridors with dim lights when they carried her in.

The large detaining room holding her bore a lone sign on its only window: Cell 33.

Carla was with perhaps fifty other young women in this seemingly all-steel room of a silvery color, with cots on the floor. This cellblock was where those held prisoner would huddle close to each other, their only protection by their proximity, on vigil scanning the corridors of different colors and dimly lit, on guard against those coming to open their cage. Tonight, her eyes were too heavy to keep open, and she succumbed to deep sleep.

She awakened when she realized her clothes were being ripped away amidst heavy breathing from strange-looking expressionless men, only to discover they looked like men but at the same time didn't seem human. Shadowy hands slipped a hospital-like gown over her.

———

At a highway Rest Stop, Sam made a call. "Major Briggs?"

"Yes?"

"It's your old Sergeant—"

"Dawson! *The* Sam Dawson?" Briggs said with surprise. "Well, I'll be...how the hell are you?"

"I've been better. How's life at Los Alamos?"

"Same ol', same ol'—Above Top Secret stuff," the Major answered in a raspy voice. "I never thought a man of war would end up in a lab full of brainy nerds, but military know-how became needed in the trenches. In three months, no more punching Uncle Sam's clock, the Missus and I retire to Hawaii." The Major caught himself. "Anything wrong?"

"I'm an hour or so away. Can we meet ASAP?"

"Sure."

In his Jeep, Sam drove southwest until he came upon a road sign reading *Los Alamos, New Mexico,* that sat on the Pajarito Plateau, the town built on a series of fingers of land called mesas, separated by deep canyons. Most of the city rested on the plateaus, around 7,500 feet above sea level. Sam knew that Los Alamos was home to the U.S. Department of Energy's national research laboratories, which delivered science and technology to protect our nation and promote world stability...whatever the hell that meant. It was also one of the top U.S. research laboratories specializing in studying the human genome.

Briggs had ordered Sam to meet far clear of Los Alamos so as not to get tangled with the intense security of one of America's highest top classified facilities. He pulled into the parking lot and went inside to spot his former superior, Major Jason Briggs, in a booth, his demeanor still rigid. They shook hands, Sam sitting across from him.

"So, did you save some civilian life for me?" Briggs asked.

"It's all yours....like watching paint dry or politicians campaign."

"How's the ticker holding up?"

"Some limitations in the beginning," Sam admitted. "Other than the defibrillator beating in my chest like King Kong, bent on kicking some ass, I'm fine. Just as long as I take precautions, like staying away from strong magnetic fields, their force can throw off the heart rhythm, often requiring the widget to be re-set."

"Why are we here, Sam?"

"Someone's taken my daughter just outside of Dulce."

A waitress interrupted to take their orders and left, and Sam gave more details.

"This is terrible," Briggs said, leaning over the table conspiratorially. "I want to help."

"What's going on at the Dulce Military Installation?"

Briggs paused, calculating his answer.

Sam immediately started. "Didn't Warfare One-O-One teach that when you're looking for a rat, you'll smell it before seeing it?"

The Major smiled, tight-lipped. "It's like the old joke: I can tell you, but then I'd have to kill you."

"Can you get me inside?" Sam asked but heard nothing but silence from across the table. "Sir, you've been a hero of mine since Korengal Valley—"

"No, you've been mine," Briggs insisted. "Mission after mission right up to that last cluster fuck."

"You told me you owed me when I became shot at because of someone else's cluster fuck. You never were one to bullshit, so help me save my daughter."

When the admiral looked away, Sam slowly rose. "Thanks a lot, sir. Sorry to bother you!"

"Sit your ass back down, soldier!"

Patrons about the diner glared their way. Sam sat as the waitress brought their food and quickly left.

Jason Briggs stirred a sugar cube into his coffee, gathering his thoughts. "There's a secret sector of the government that's a big nasty business. They preside over our country's too-tough-to-handle bin. Dulce's Underground Military Installation is so secret its existence is one of the least known in the world. So sensitive that it's doubtful the

President of the United States knows much about what goes on inside. They want to keep it that way."

"They? Who are they?"

Sam knew the mantra well, reciting it speedily. "Answer to no one, do what you must, as long as no dirt trails back to the White House, right? Because this is a democracy, and that means the public is too stupid to understand, right? That's why we're fighting how many wars?"

"Same ol' Sam," Briggs said with an all-knowing grin. "So you understand the shit you'd stir up trying to penetrate Dulce?"

"I'd clean it up once I have my daughter back."

"You can't get in there, Sam. You'll get yourself killed."

"If Carla's inside, I'll take my chances."

Briggs considered this. "If you start something that leads back to me, I'll retire in Arlington Cemetery instead of Hawaii!"

"I need something, *anything* that'll help!"

"Don't you get it? You'll have the CIA, FBI, and other alphabet names after you!"

"Tell them good luck. Have a good time in Hawaii, sir." Sam said defiantly and stomped out of the diner.

The Major got on his cell and dialed. "Sir, we're about to have a situation."

———

Sam drove back to his lonely mountain cabin outside of Dulce, unable to stop thinking of Major Briggs. Something about him was different than the guy he once knew. Everyone changes; that's a part of life, and Sam knew the civilian version of himself was a far cry from the soldiering one. What was more disconcerting about Briggs was that the one in battle quickly responded to a situation and answered. The Jason Briggs he'd just met paused uncharacteristically indecisive.

Some leaders had an inner motor that pushed them to get to the heart of an issue and find solutions. That was Major Briggs. He would drill for specific answers, only giving up once he got them. His *high energy* was infectious. The Briggs of old would've searched tenaciously for information, pulling out all stops to help Sam find his daughter. This current version of Briggs reminded Sam of a T.V. newscast coming in from some part of the world, with a bit of lag time as they waited to hear the question that the audience at home had already heard. Strangely, Briggs was waiting to hear how to respond to Sam's question, like an older person with a lag time in his mind.

Sam dreaded calling his ex-wife but had to dial. "Did you find her?" Hearing a pause sent Karen into a panic. "Oh, God...what? Tell me!"

"Nothing yet. You still have that friend at the V.A.?"

"Uh, yeah. Why?"

"Need info on a Harry Hatchet Chalma," Sam directed. "He might still live on the Jicarilla Apache reservation in New Mexico. Should be getting benefits."

"Okay, what else?"

"Find everything you can about a military base on that Indian Res called Dulce. D-u-l-c-e."

"I don't understand. What has this got—"

"Do it. There is also chatter, gibberish, and social media about what happens there. Oh, and if it's connected to the Los Alamos Laboratories."

———

Boulder, Colorado

Two-star General Nathan Blake activated the safety measure monitors that secured his home in a luxury suburban complex, tucking it away for the night. A bluish-tint from a half dozen monitors eerily lit the small security room. This authoritative, tightly wound billiard ball bald man in his early sixties had a diet of fried eggs, black coffee, and cigarettes and was a heavy drinker. However, he was always aware of his surroundings and could defend himself if attacked. His frequent exposure to death helped lead to his cynical and callous attitude. That type of demeanor was part of his armor for being the supreme commander in America's Deep Underground Military Bases worldwide called "DUMBs."

General Blake bypassed the grand living area to go downstairs to his study, securing the door behind him. He unlocked a file cabinet to take out two artists rendering collage drawings of today's world. One was of industries belching out thick smoke, log jams of traffic paralyzing big cities, endless eye-sore power line wires leading to and from huge, flashy facilities, and giant shovels digging into Mother Earth as if eating the planet alive. It left gaping holes everywhere, rain forests as trees crashed. Mammoth-sized rigs sucking the world dry of oil, and millions, if not billions, of people cramming into big cities.

The other artist's rendering depicted a far different version of Earth. This perfect world had the look of natural beauty: lush greenness, a total lack of telephone and other communication wires, traffic-free roads as people moved about on electromagnetic machines, solar, wind, and ocean power creating energy without the use of oil-burning machinery, simmering volcanoes tapped into for non-stop thermal control. The big city streets had far, far fewer people. In the photo's background was a bottomless pit, dead bodies being tossed into it and bulldozed over.

"They promise a great day for the planet when the plan becomes completed," Blake said, smoothing a hand over his silver hair. He knew it was too late for anyone or any group to halt the future crime against humanity. Depopulation was a significant part of the agenda.

One of the private phones buzzed.

"Line clear?" Blake asked.

"Yes, General. We have a situation."

Blake listened as the voice detailed the situation.

"Yes, sir, tomorrow." General Blake ended the call, a chill running down his spine as he left the room. Thoughts of "The Plan" followed him, a strategy so evil, racist, sinister, and massive that it defied belief. Its disclosure could only happen once it was too late to stop it. Many committed citizens had lost their lives trying to lift the veil of secrecy.

Early in the morning the following day, General Blake kissed his wife, leaving his house, appearing just like any other husband going to work. A government sedan drove him to the Denver International Airport. He was boarding a flight but chose to walk through the modern concourse of the terminal, passing a series of murals that ranged in intensity from unnerving to apocalyptically creepy.

The two-star General found two murals that detailed The Plan for a New World Order. The first depicted a giant Nazi-like soldier with dead women and children scattered around him. The second showed Third World populations dying, but some elite had protection from the day of reckoning in sealed containers.

Blake liked the sheer audacity of the fresco, a presumption the conspirators chose to publicly announce their Machiavellian plans by putting this out there for everyone to see. *Now, this is confidence*, Blake thought. *Nothing could stop The Plan.*

The General made it to Concourse C and a militarized intermediary entrance in the United Airlines section. He opened a door after punching in the door code "BE64B," knowing it by heart.

A shuttle train took him through a three-mile-long tunnel headed out from the intermediary entrance to a full-blown sanctioned militarized hall nestled in five buildings one hundred and twenty feet beneath the surface. Below it were eight cities virtually stacked on one another.

General Blake got aboard a Mach 2 maglev train, TAUSS—the Trans America Underground Subway System. The train magnetically levitated an inch above the tracks, resisting further friction. Zipping from Denver at nearly fifteen hundred miles an hour, he made it to Las Alamos—the world's largest and most advanced bio-genetic facility in less than half an hour.

Blake, driven through a vehicular tunnel, took him off the ultra-restricted Los Alamos area to a lone small mountain. He became led to a massive vaulted steel door. It was so large it made one wonder if giants were to inhabit beyond the door's other side. The door's locking devices were operable from the inside, only protected against any possible damage by blast action against the outside surface of the doors. In keeping with those instructions, large wheel handles fitted inside the two more oversized doors, each two feet thick and weighing two tons. Yet the entry, so delicately balanced, could open and close by applying a mere fifty pounds of force against their bulk. Placing the handle on the inside served two functions. First, it enabled those inside the facility to lock themselves in against those who might otherwise try to enter. It protected the locking mechanism from a blast. The door was also to protect those inside from unwanted people from intruding. Turning the handle one way, giant pins or rollers slid into fittings behind the frame. Turning the wheel the other way released the pins. Not surprisingly, the whole apparatus resembled the workings of a safe— but instead of deterring robbers, it could withstand an atomic explosion.

While a new ski resort just built atop Pajarito Ski Mountain with beautiful views of Los Alamos, the Sangre de Cristo, and Jemez mountains provided a disguise for a secret government company. They could haul three thousand loads to the site and pour 40,000 tons of concrete into fissures leading into the underworld empire.

General Blake's trip through the tunnel way of the deep underground base passed walls three feet thick and reinforced with steel. The ultra-intricate air intake system became explicitly designed to filter out radiation and create a vacuum-like effect when you walk in. The wind howled around you and sucked all the doors shut. The entire structure, the size of two Wal-Marts, was covered with a concrete roof and buried beneath forty feet of dirt.

The 60,000-square-foot bunker built one thousand feet into the hillside had no outdoor entrances except the one connecting to the Las Alamos laboratory. However, it did have one secret exit in case of extreme emergency. The facility featured decontamination chambers, a power plant, water storage tanks, an air filtering system, a clinic with operating rooms, a pharmacy, dormitories, and food supplies for three years to accommodate more than two thousand people—the "survivors." These chosen ones would also have radio and communication equipment to message other survival groups about the country and world.

Blake proceeded to the Deep Underground Command Center (DUCC) and its state-of-the-art Situation Room retreat. An elevator took him to the most critical alert and intelligence center in the southwest American desert. "The Tank," as it was known, was filled with high-tech gadgetry and one-hundred and fifty monitor screens on surveillance at U.S. DUMB activities in real-time.

The seemingly unending screens about The Tank had location names under each: Alaska, Area 51, Groom Lake, Deep Springs, California, Denver, Dulce, Greenbrier, Washington D.C., and Montauk among the list of over one hundred and fifty bases. Most of them were in virtually every major city or nearby. The DUMBs were over a mile underground, the walls two-feet thick and reinforced with steel. At each entrance, cranes hung humongous steel doors and to have a range of five to ten miles across, with several considerably larger, all inter-connected by high-speed train. Later, the entire system became covered with a concrete roof and buried beneath twenty feet of dirt.

CHAPTER 5

Inside The Tank's cavernous room, General Blake met Major Briggs and ten other apostles of their "Shadow Group." Two governments were in the United States today. One was visible; another was this invisible Dirty Dozen group, merely a shadow. The first was the government that citizens read about in newspapers and their children studied about in civics books. The second was the highly secretive, interlocking agencies that carried out hidden agendas, the Shadow Group at the forefront.

This international team that the Chairman of the Board, General Blake, presided over was powerful, brutally violent, and treacherous. They had operatives in the academic world, in intelligence agencies, in the military (both officers and enlisted personnel), in private industry, in the world of corporate and public sector high finance bankers, financiers, and industrialists, in the new media, religions, the list went on. The Shadow Group had powerful connections in dozens of countries worldwide and could overthrow and influence governments almost immediately. It was a sprawling octopus with the United States and the world in its deadly grasp.

Of the one hundred most significant economies in the world, fifty-one were corporations, while only forty-nine were countries. The Shadow Group had their fingers in every fifty-one of these multi-national corporations.

Each member passed through an X-ray-type machine, which strangely scanned only their heads. Sam Dawson's visage appeared on a wall screen as the group sat on a large

U-shaped table. He received a medal from Major Briggs and gave an acceptance speech, ending with, "…It's been an honor to serve my country. I'm proud to have stood by my oath of enlistment that I will support and defend the Constitution of the United States against all enemies, foreign and domestic; that I will bear true faith and allegiance to the same; and that I will obey the orders of the President of the United States and orders—"

General Blake freeze-framed the screen on Dawson's face. "So Dawson won't back off?"

"No sir," Major Briggs answered. "He's a father looking for his daughter, sir, nothing more."

"You two were close?"

"Very."

"You said he was a killing machine?" Blake asked.

"The highest rank for unorthodox covert operations, best Special Forces soldier I ever trained, a legend," Briggs assessed. "Ultra-proven in combat, never asking his men to do anything he wasn't ready to do or left behind, things that made him quite popular with his men. The only problem for the command chain was Dawson's reputation as a loose cannon."

"How so?" the General asked.

"He didn't follow orders that he didn't think were in the best interest of his men—a fact that just made him more popular with them," the Major answered. "A special breed of warrior, a common person with a uniquely uncommon desire to succeed."

"You don't say," Blake said before finishing his coffee.

"Dawson's missions were always so top secret that no one knew all the details," Briggs breathed deeply before asking, "Did they abduct his daughter?"

"Who knows?" a businessman asked. "They've been

snatching whomever they want for so long; they could have fucking Elvis!"

A nerdy-looking scientist with a helium-type voice said, "They can also take Mick Jagger's Rolling Stones and Homer Simpson, as long as they keep giving us our products!"

The group chuckled over the remark before Major Briggs spoke again. "There's something else about Dawson. His post-traumatic stress is so acute that the docs label him a tripwire soldier. He's had several assault charges pressed against him."

Sam had had several fights with civilian macho guys, wanting to test precisely how tough a Special Forces soldier was. One of the men with a double jaw fracture claimed Sam, in a bar brawl, sucker punched him. However, a waitress testified that that wasn't the case; the civilian swung at Sam from behind but missed. There were other civilian fights, but the one telling on his marriage was Sam beating up a man to within an inch of his life when found in bed with his wife, Carla, sleeping in another room.

Briggs added, "Two psychiatrists deduce that when an injury forced him to retire, leaving the battle zone for the pacifist civilian life brought on for him suicidal tendencies."

Blake took on a wry smile. "Well, if he self-destructs, he won't be a problem anymore."

These above-the-law members nodded in agreement, but that was Sam Dawson's problem, not theirs. The Shadow Group's movement had begun over fifty years ago when those controlling them convinced the forbears of this above-the-law group that many things were wrong with the world. Blake and his apostles would assume critical positions once they accomplished a more orderly world. They ruled the government.

Blake waved his hand to the group. "Let's rewind to

Sam Dawson. There's a saying in the military: if you bring me a problem, bring me a solution."

"He has to disappear!" the scientist continued.

"Isn't there another way?" Briggs asked with concern.

The General shot him a glare. "You know the answer. Nothing, absolutely nothing, must get in our way. If Dulce gets breached and secrets exposed, the installation and all the inhabitants will be blown to bits, erasing all evidence. There is a Plan set. Nothing must alter it."

Major Briggs became visibly upset but nodded in understanding. He left with the others, except Blake, whose instincts gave off warning signals. Something wasn't right with the Major; he was still softhearted toward Dawson. Blake knew how Dawson had saved his life at Korangal Valley in north-eastern Afghanistan—often called the Valley of Death. Though the Major had been several miles away giving Sam's squad Intel against the insurgent Taliban, Sam learned of Briggs' command post next in line to be raided and then bombed. When communication broke down, Sam risked life and limb to navigate through hostile terrain—a gauntlet of fire—to reach Briggs to get him out of harm's way. Two minutes later, the raid came, no officers at all, and missiles flattened the command post.

General Blake went back on communication. "Monitor Briggs...who he meets, his communications."

———

Another government sedan pulled into the driveway, its driver opening the door for Major Briggs, and then the sedan left. Briggs went inside his Los Alamos area, a home of traditional elegance, and kissed his wife. She stirred and smiled, but her eyes stayed closed. A book, *The Good Life in Hawaii,* was on the bed by her side. The clock showed 11 pm.

Briggs knew that the two had a spot to build a home

that no one, absolutely no one, knew about, their plan to escape everyone and everything. The Major changed into a robe and slippers and moved into the library room, pouring scotch from a crystal decanter into a snifter glass. Briggs lit a cigar before viewing the distinguished portraits covering the walls: Presidents Truman, Eisenhower, and others. He reflected on a photo of himself with a uniformed Sergeant Sam Dawson, pinning another medal on him.

"I owe you, soldier," he said softly to Sam's image.

The Major took out two tiny magnets, shaped like dimes, though smaller and thicker at one-quarter inch. He tested them by putting each atop a medal paper holder that quickly lifted the five-pounds. Taking out a small compass to find the north side, he placed the magnets to face his skin before attaching them to a strip of tape across the bridge of his nose, holding them into place.

Briggs sat sipping scotch, contemplating the gravity of what he was about to do. He wasn't a crazy or vengeful malcontent, just a man who must step forward to tell the truth, a harsh truth that represents a failure on everybody's part, including his. The Major had to do it for the country Briggs cared for more than himself. No one had to tell him he'd strayed from becoming a misguided soul, catching himself in the middle of worshipping these demon gods like others in the Shadow Group had succumbed to, their minds becoming altered beyond recognition. He knew the demon gods' modus operandi: to make it appear that nothing was happening. However, Briggs knew otherwise and that the ones controlling them would stop at nothing to achieve their goals.

Two hours later, the sounds diminished in Brigg's mind, relegated to static before he heard anything. Knowing he had to work fast, he began writing longhand on a legal pad with a shaky hand. Twenty minutes tops were all he had. His microchip could go awry and draw suspicion from the Controllers monitoring his movements, hearing and recording his conversations along with those, whom he talked to, transmitting voices either into his brain or his inner ear, even fucking reading his thoughts. He wished he could generate awareness among the American public that what he was going through was honest and could happen to anyone. And also, it was a death sentence for him or any other Silent Group members to leak this publicly.

Briggs set his wristwatch on the table alongside him and jotted down the time. Knowing the value of documentation, he wrote a paragraph on the sheet and read it aloud. "This letter is for the three people I trust most in life. As I do, they want the best for all Americans: my wife Jen, former Special Forces soldier Sam Dawson, and Senator Paul McNair. Should I disappear or die in mysterious circumstances or be accused of some crime I haven't committed, my wife (who will know nothing of this letter until its release) will instruct her to send this document to Dawson and McNair. May your conscience be your guide over what to do with these following accusations of mine."

Jason Briggs continued his confession. "I am a Shadow Group member or forced to be. What I signed on for is not what's going on today. The government lied to me and everyone for almost sixty years and thus must continue the lie. One lie used to cover another, and now it's become impossible to come clean."

He admitted having undergone several security tests, one of which was hypnosis. While under, he was unaware of being microchipped.

"In a nutshell, the planet is getting controlled by an off-world species," Briggs wrote. "A few species are forcing humans into a gene pool to get their species back up and running. The deal we made with them for their advanced technology — allowing them to experiment on a few humans — has gone awry. They're snatching humans comparable to vampires in the night. It's a wonder anyone 'in the know' can sleep at night."

Briggs concentrated on the wording of another admission. "A major finding of the alien study was that the government could not tell the public since this knowledge most certainly would lead to economic collapse, the collapse of the religious structure, and national panic, leading to anarchy. That could happen, and what *will* happen if we do nothing to try and stop this complete takeover."

The Major's subsequent admission was even more appalling. "The Shadow Group is working with this controller group that has infiltrated every major government on the planet. Within a year or two, the Shadow Great Plan will implement — accomplishing a more orderly curtailed world in which the elitists would rule."

Briggs continued pouring forth an expose' of misdeeds by the Shadow Group. "These mentioned two spots warrant a close examination. Breaking their codes and symbols will have one seeing a symbolic opening into The Plan. The names of the elitist Shadow Group that see themselves as having the divine right as the world's caretakers and its rulers who feel it's right for them to execute The Controller Plan to eliminate a large proportion of the world's populations — nearly *ninety percent*! The above alien species is pulling the strings behind this dastardly move. Thanks to technology, they don't need 320,000,000 million Americans to run their system; they need only 32,000,000. They view the rest of Americans as 'useless eaters' needing 'culled' from society, much like animals in a herd killed to make the group better and stronger.

"This admission, put in a letter instead of me speaking publicly, may seem to be a cowardly approach that I should outright blow the whistle on the Shadow Group's heinous plan to unleash on the planet. I do fear for my life and also my wife's. If these power elitists knew what I'm now admitting, neither of us would ever see the light of day again."

Briggs included more particulars before noting the time — eighteen minutes had gone by — two minutes under the allotted safety time, and he finished a sentence before seating his pen down. He wanted to document so much more, but further revelations would have to wait another day and let some time pass. On the coffee table were several phones, one of which was red. He lifted the receiver to a black phone.

Sam, sleeping in his cabin, was awakened by his ringing cell. "Dawson, Major Briggs."

"Yes, sir?"

"Watch your back, soldier."

"I'm a marked man?"

"Targeted for elimination. Do not communicate with me again. Good luck, soldier. May God be on your side."

Briggs hung up, took the magnet strip from his nose, and sat again gazing at the photo of Dawson and him. Several minutes later, he heard the soft, distant sound of voices in his head returning, the device controlling him re-activated.

———

The line went dead. Sam threw his belongings into a duffel bag and saw a bottle of Jack Daniels, his only dear friend of late, on the shelf. "Sorry, Jack, shit happens. It's been good." He broke the seal and poured Jack out the window, ingesting a heart pill instead. "Sorry, my friend, but we have to part for a while so I can keep sharp."

Once he got onto the main road toward Dulce, Sam saw a black Lincoln Town car concealed in the pines pulled out. "You fuckers are getting on my nerves."

His juices began to flow, activating battle instincts stored in mothballs. Sam took several turns, lost the car, and then located the Gilmore efficiency apartments with a "Vacancy" sign outside. He pulled into the lot and headed to the front desk to register.

Sam entered his spare efficiency one-room apartment with a double bed, a small desk, a T.V., a small closet, and a bathroom. He unpacked his belongings, including Carla's computer, and then moved about setting some clever Special Forces devices meant to detect potential breaches. Anything moved or touched in his apartment would leave a tell-tale sign. Sam would be notified on his cell phone when it saw a body or heat motion, allowing him to hear what was happening inside his room.

After setting another breach device, he made a call.
"Sam Dawson."
"Shit, guy," Sheriff Wilson said. "It's after midnight."
"Sorry, I can't sleep. Got anything for me?"
"Nothin' yet, but the search goes on."
"I'm staying at the Gilmore Apartments, not leaving without Carla."
"Figured as much."
"Oh…you deal with the Jicarilla Indians here, right?"
"Some. What d'ya need?"
"Ever hear of an Apache named Harry?"
"Doesn't ring a bell. His last name?"
Sam was about to give the last name Chama when the room's curtain window cracked. He saw a black patrol sedan cruising by. He changed his mind. "Nah. My memory's shot. I think he's an Indian. If he's not living on the Res, right off it."
"Well, keep the faith. We gotta bigger net out there to find your girl."

"Thanks."

Sam opened the door a crack but waited minutes before stepping out. The Lincoln Town car was gone. All appeared clear. He changed into camouflage fatigues, ready for the night, packed things in his vehicle, and left. The adrenaline from his release valve began to flow faster, the thrill of the chase in his nostrils. However, he corralled his excitement, well aware that the game of chess players would be deliberate. No foolish moves could end the contest for him, his life.

He drove through the desolate town and into the Reservation countryside. Finding a secure spot off the road amongst boulders, he slept in his car, knowing he'd need it. He didn't go into a slumber but worked to get himself into the warrior mindset. He began to focus on his former training designed to be uncomfortable — physically first, then mentally. That was what he'd done to take him and other Special Forces soldiers to dark places under control so that if they were ever brought there by the enemy, it wouldn't be their first time. He stared into the darkness, trying to visualize this new battlefield by integrating all five senses. He knew that he saw, heard, smelled, touched, and tasted would all come into play when the game ratcheted.

There was an old saying that if you think you're in danger, sleep with one eye open. Taking the adage literally, Sam had spent excessive time studying ducks and dolphins that could control which side of the brain stayed awake and which one dozed while sleeping. He was far from being an expert at this as they were, but he deduced that only a few humans could do it with the skill he'd mastered.

The rising sun awakened part of Sam's sleep. So much had gone on in the last two days, and all he knew for sure was his daughter was still missing; he was a marked man. He headed towards town, but as soon as he got onto the main road, he put his magnum on the passenger seat to drive with one hand.

Sam glanced into his rearview mirror, seeing one of the vans moving into the passing lane, the back window sliding down, and another dark-attired Rock Man sticking out an Uzi gun. Sam swerved, bumping the van into a drainage ditch. His heart began thumping amidst heavy breathing; he heard a guardian angel from hell whispering, *You miss war, do you? Well, it misses you!*

A dust storm behind him kicked out of nowhere, and a herd of Big Horn Elk stampeded across the road. Some even stopped on the asphalt as if putting up a roadblock for those pursuing Sam; the vans in pursuit slammed on their brakes, tires screeching, unable to precede chasing Sam until the herd passed through. When they finally did, Sam's vehicle turned into a tiny dot in the distance until it disappeared altogether.

CHAPTER 6

After the incident and being unable to locate their quarry, the vans parked along the roadside, and the elk herd was gone as quickly as they appeared.

A Rock security man inside one of the vehicles carrying advanced weaponry took out his phone. "We missed him. Something weird happened."

General Blake didn't like what he was hearing. "Don't give me weird! Give me *dead!*"

———

Sam pulled off the road and fantasized about eating his once-in-a-blue-moon McDonald's fast food breakfast, but with danger lurking, he had to settle for military rations. His cell rang. He recognized the number and picked it up. "Karen, don't call me on this number again while I get a new cell. Use e-mail, but don't look for my usual name."

"Someone's after you, right?"

"Don't know. What do you have?"

Karen had come through. "Dulce, New Mexico. There are rumors of medical experiments at their Biogenetics Base — lots of other weird, gory stuff online, the usual conspiracy websites everyone laughs at, but some are scary beyond belief. Like below Archuleta Mesa, the home to Nightmare Hall!"

"What's that about?" Sam asked.

"I don't know, but it's all about horror and carnage, stuff that makes Doctor Frankenstein appear to be a Disney character." His ex's voice tightened. "Talk of ongoing human and animal mutilations. It is difficult to sift through mountains of speculation to find hard facts. However, the town has been the epicenter for nearly every paranormal activity one can imagine." Karen panicked. "Find my girl!"

"*Our* girl! I will."

"Can't someone in the government help you?"

"I don't know who to trust on this one. And, by the way, you were always in my thoughts."

"But second in your heart, I know," she lamented. "Look, I found your Harry Chama, aka Hatchet. His checks get sent to another tribe near the reservation named Nantan Lupan, which means Grey Wolf. This Hatchet man of yours has an R.D. 1 address and gets his mail at the reservation post office."

"Good work," Sam said. "Gotta go, talk soon."

It's just a matter of scheduling. Sam drove on as that suicidal part of him thought we were all on this planet and death row. He also believed he could face his check-out time ready and willing, even push forward his departure. That all changed when instincts told him that some deranged group had taken his Carla. Sam wasn't much for praying, but as he drove on, he asked the Lord not to take him until his little girl was safe.

Sam eventually located Harry at a ranch where cattle roamed outside a corral, work trucks about, and the Archuleta mesa looming at roughly 9000 feet in elevation, rising over the high desert town of Dulce by more than 2,600 feet. He drove up to the main house and saw Harry Hatchet moving about with a noticeable limp souvenir from his war days, working with two teenage boys lifting hay bales onto a flatbed truck. An unsmiling Sam got out and approached.

Hatchet was quite surprised. "Sarge?"

Sam skipped niceties and got into his face. "I got a big problem, Hatchet, that has me ready to flush the toilet on your tribe!"

"Nice to see you too—"

Sam grabbed his collars to pin him against the flatbed. The teens moved in, one pointing a pitchfork at him.

"Stop it!" one teen boy yelled, sparring with the sharp tool and threatening to stab this aggressor.

Sam released his grip and took out the two Indian feathers. "These were found next to her car. My daughter went missing two days ago on his Res. Sheriff Wilson or whatever said they belong to your tribe. Start talking!"

"I followed you into battle; you saved my life. Believe that this isn't the first time we Indians are getting set up."

"Get to the point, soldier."

"They want to blame us—you know—those stupid, hopped-up Injuns!" Harry Hatchet said with deep disdain. "All the weird shit happenin' on the Res is because of us!" He glanced at his sons. "It's okay; leave us alone."

The curious boys drifted off toward the barn.

"Give me a hand so my sons can feed some hungry cattle. And I'll get you up to speed."

Lifting bales onto the flatbed, Hatchet listened to what had happened to Sam's daughter, his expression growing grim. He admitted that local Apaches had often reported strange lights in the sky, especially around the high number of cattle mutilations in that area over the past few years.

"My uncle's ranch has a canyon," Hatchet went on, "really long, and the cows grazed way up at the end. Something chased one down because you could see where it ran into the brush. It died; where it lay, there were three holes in the ground but no tracks, and that cow had no blood. My uncle returned there the next day, and the cow's internal organs were gone, and the udders burned out. Some real weird shit, hell, the cows wouldn't go back up there."

"Fuck the cows," Sam seethed. "I want my daughter!"

"Around here, there are lots of missing people, mostly teens, who disappear without a trace," Hatchet admitted. "As soon as you try to get close to the truth, Rock men in black come visitin' you, and your life will change forever at this time."

"Is there some kind of abduction thing going on inside Archuleta?" Sam asked. "What the?" he noticed an odd-looking animal hopping toward a small mesa nearby, appearing to be half rabbit/half cat with large jack-rabbit hind legs and long ears.

"We call 'em Cabbits, a mixture of rabbit and cat."

"I didn't know they could cross-breed."

"They can't. But a lot of high desert strangeness has been goin' on for decades. You never know what is what, who's who."

"What about the residents? How many work in the base?"

"None of 'em," Hatchet answered. "There are those not from this area in the last few decades. Why here, of all places, Apaches could never understand."

"I saw teens in town, a set of twins acting strange."

"Were they wearing sunglasses?" Sam nodded. "We Injuns don't trust any of 'em," Hatchet admitted. "They work at gas stations, drugstores, and bars; their kids attend school. Even Sheriff Wilson is questionable."

"How so?"

"He's been sheriff for five or so years, but lately actin' different, like it's him but isn't if you know what I mean. I can't prove it; hell, no one can. But many believe they're listening and reporting anything violating the base's security limit."

"Like those goons in black suits riding in tinted glass government vans?"

Harry Hatchet nodded. "Rock men are security guys who pressure curious passersby until they escort their vehicle out of Dodge. There's been a story of UFO hunter people resisting leaving. Two disappeared, never to be seen or heard from again."

Hatchet described Dulce as second only to Roswell, New Mexico, in people seeking more proof of off-world species. Although Roswell was far more popular because of the famed supposed UFO crash in 1947, Dulce was the more sinister, with a high rate of cattle mutations and human abductions that Roswell had none of that.

The two former soldiers had finished loading when Hatchet introduced his sons to Sam before they drove off with the grass.

"What about our good Major?"

"Strange what you said about some people acting strange around here," Sam answered. "The Briggs I met isn't the one we used to know. It's like he has a lag time when answering a question. Maybe the beginnings of Alzheimer's, or did he have a stroke? I don't know."

"I hope he's alright. He must be because he's heavily into underground military bases."

"DUMBs," Sam informed, knowing the acronym.

"Dulce would have to be one 'cause there's not much to the base on the surface," Hatchet assessed. "I heard it's a program called 'Beyond Black'...Need-to-Know clearance."

"Ah, the old drill: Absolute secrecy and rigorous security procedures have been established and are the absolute rule, with any significant breeches typically followed by termination with extreme prejudice."

"Roger that."

They recalled what they'd heard while enlisted. In 2001, Secretary of Defense Donald Rumsfeld's speech mentioned that the Pentagon had lost 2.3 trillion dollars! Where did it go? The top secret Military Space Program? Black projects? The spending on these top-secret projects went beyond Congressional oversight.

"Betcha a huge chunk of those trillions is for building DUMB bases," Hatchet assessed.

Sam thought about that. "So the sixty-four-thousand-dollar question: what does Briggs know about Dulce?"

"I bet plenty. Rumor is that underground trains connect it to Las Alamos and other joint bases."

"*Joint* is the keyword," Sam deduced. "Who's our government in joint intelligence with those inside Dulce?"

"Nothing would surprise me," Hatchet said. "That in Indian lore, Las Alamos was the Dark Cloud on the horizon. The North American tribes had quite a philosophy about it that nothing of grace was there. Add to that, Dulce; its strangeness smells of something pure and sinister."

"Briggs stuck his neck out, warning me," Sam said. "He wants to tell me what's happening, but his hands are tied."

"I wish we knew the big secret," Hatchet said.

Sam changed the subject. "Yesterday, I ran into an old Indian with a German shepherd who mentioned Archuleta as the place and called it the Rock."

"We believe so," Hatchet admitted, "but Apaches and other tribes here leave it alone."

"Why?"

"People who get too curious about the base often disappear. That Injun you ran into Billy — his wife vanished years ago, right from their backyard garden. No foottracks or tire marks. Never found."

That admission brought on a massive wave of angst overtaking Sam. "Can you help me get inside the place?" Hatchet became silent. "For fuck's sake, this is my daughter!

She's in danger! They tried to kill me on my way here."

"Who?"

"Rock security men in black vans chasing me with Uzis locked me in."

"Whoa," Hatchet said, shocked. "I know they're around to listen, report, and act upon anything that violates base security, but Uzis?"

"I thought I just bought the farm," Sam admitted, "until a herd of elk coming out of nowhere crossed the road to block their way, allowing me to escape."

"Oh...it's serious now. Elk, you say?"

"Yeah. So?"

"Best we hide your wheels." Hatchet saw Sam take his bow from the car. "The old Indian you saw yesterday, I guess you could call him our Medicine Man, full of superstitions and odd cures. Some say a part of his mind flew over the cuckoo's nest. Others, me included, believe the ol' codger is smarter than anyone thinks, along with his healing powers."

"Well, I got something needing curing," Sam said threateningly. "Hope your Medicine Man can work his magic."

CHAPTER 7

In the belly of Archuleta Mesa, a super elevator transported Roger and several other guards wearing jumpsuits, blank expressions, not talking to one another, arriving for the shift change. The shape of the elevator was unique—like a Tupperware sugar bowl, an open-ended oval with another half oval on each side. The elevator shaft matched the form perfectly. The magnetic controls were half-oval in shape.

Roger, closest to the magnets, could feel the slight pull of their power. The elevator was smooth and silent; a nearly unnoticed surge occurred when the movement started or stopped. There were no cables because the lift was not electric, and the magnets were ultra-powerful.

The elevator stopped on Level Five. The doors hissed open, and the guards disembarked into a futuristic area. The tunnels seemed endless and had subdued colored lighting with a purplish hue created from chemo-luminescence all along the upper and lower sections of the walls.

A Maglev-type train left the station transporting expressionless workers in jumpsuits of various colors.

The guards stripped naked to line up at a scale to get weighed. Their card had to match the weight and code, or the door wouldn't open. Any weight discrepancy, any change over three pounds, would summon security since no one was allowed to carry anything in or out of the sensitive areas. A green light signaled, allowing the men passage. Roger went to a locker room to put on a different colored jumpsuit with a breast symbol of an upside-down black triangle with the inverted gold colored T. Also about were symbols and words not derived from an earthly language, somewhat like hieroglyphics but still unique all to its own.

This human guard walked along one corridor to begin his day's work and noticed the usual mysterious, omnipresent beings in the nearby shadows observing the machinations. Roger had been working here for a couple of years, and still, he couldn't get over being spooked by these creepy things in the shadows that he never saw up close.

The Guards passed clearance and lined up to receive small glass vials filled with a red blood-like solution. They eagerly drank them.

––––––––––

Harry Hatchet drove his pickup truck along a dirt road and saw a Rock van advancing from the opposite direction, slowing its speed to study who was inside before it continued. On the truck's flatbed, Sam lay concealed by bales of hay. Hatchet banged on the trailer door when it pulled into a desolate area. Sam climbed from the grass to find a German shepherd growling at him. Old Billy came over.

"Can you speak some English with us, Billy?" Hatchet asked.

"Depends."

"You know my daughter's missing," Sam said. "Can you help me find her?"

Billy studied the white man's face as Hatchet gestured to Sam's bow. "He's good with this."

"Our brave warrior used a bow to slay the Sky People."

"Sky People?" Sam asked.

"Sam Dawson was my sergeant in Afghanistan," Hatchet said. "A herd of Big Horn Elk saved him when Rock men tried to kill him."

Billy's eyes lit up. "You don't say? Could he be the

one?"

"One what?"

Neither Indian answered.

Billy became Hatchet's passenger in his truck when they saw another patrol van approaching and again scrutinizing the vehicle before moving on. Ten minutes later, Hatchet pulled onto a road leading to the imposing Archuleta Mesa. He parked at a barely visible roadway overgrown with bushes and banged on the outside of his door, which had Sam coming out from the hay pile to join them outside the truck. Billy pointed to the road leading directly to the peak, overgrown with weeds.

"Many moons ago," he said, "the strange ones dug this road through to mountain...White Men claimed for a lumber company. Trucks go in and out for a long time. Then, the road was blocked and destroyed. The signs on the trucks were Smith Corporation, out of Pagosa Springs, Colorado. Bull! Never saw any lumber comin' out jus' strange lookin' *big* machines goin' in."

"To build what?" Sam asked.

Hatchet answered, "If you lock me up for saying what I'm about to say, then you'd better lock up half us Injuns. A lifetime of silence has been goin' on behind the Dulce Base doors. Like something from another world, with our government's approval. Someone's takin' unwilling human guinea pigs from the general population. Some believe they perform experiments on captives; others heard they implant devices in their heads and bodies to control them. No doubt they have other ways to have power over their workforce."

Sam weighed this. "Again, help me get in there."

"Take out your bow," Billy instructed.

"Why?"

"Wanna see if you can hit that ol' tree up there where

the trunk bends like my crooked back."

A perplexed Sam eyed the tree, and he released the arrow. It struck precisely into the gnarled trunk. Nearby, a majestic Big Horn Elk with expansive antlers, startled by the arrow whizzing, came out from behind shrubbery to let out a bellow.

"Betcha, you can't kill it."

Sam took out another arrow and locked his sights on the elk. But again, his hands shook so badly that he lowered the bow. "I could, but I won't."

Instead, he shot again at the gnarled tree, splitting the embedded arrow.

"So you say," Billy said with a grin to Lone Wolf.

"What's going on here?"

"There's a reason you couldn't drop that elk."

"I chose not to, that's all."

Billy's cowboy boot scuffed at the parched ground, kicking up powder-like dirt. "Don't think so. Forty years ago, my wife, pregnant with our first, was out in the garden and disappeared. Never seen again."

"Is there a connection between her and my daughter?"

"Maybe. All these years, I stayed 'round here hoping they'll return my woman." Billy Two Snakes surveyed the barren land he called home.

"Hoping doesn't work for me," Sam said.

"Is that so?" Billy asked. "Climb the Rock with me tonight to begin understanding Archuleta Mesa."

———————

Dulce Installation Base

Deep inside Archuleta Mesa's DUMB, men dispersed in various directions. No matter which way they moved about, signs on doors and hallways were in an alien symbol language. Several near the train super shuttle were in English, with arrows pointing to *Area 51, Groom Lake, Los Alamos,* and other locations.

Joining Roger was a tall, very human-looking Hubrid with striking, gentle eyes, perhaps thirty years old, but hard to tell. This offspring involved splicing a human egg and sperm and adding genetic material from Hybrids-2 or 1. This ultra-rare late-stage Hubrid-3 possessed the physical and emotional mixture so close to humans that they could easily pass for one. He had honey-colored skin, sharp features, and brown hair—a beautifully androgynous mix of a man with steely strength in his tall, wiry body. He paused before speaking thoughtfully and analytically. *They want another, he* conveyed to Roger mind-to-mind without moving his lips.

"There you go again, El-Te," Roger said. "Heard ya in my mind without you speakin'...a damn ventriloquist you are." A thought hit him. "Now I know who you remind me of—Mister Spock in the *Star Trek movies!*"

"I don't know of this Spock," El-Te answered, his voice low and soft, the words spaced out for effect.

"He's a major science fiction guy. Like you, Spock controls his emotions and feels more human than his alien Vulcan part, so he has big, pointed ears."

"A Vulcan with pointy ears, hmmm," El-Te commented.

"Yeah, the movie travels an alternated parallel Star Trek universe, goin' where no man has gone before."

El-Te attempted rare humor, "Unlike me, who hasn't gone anywhere in the world beyond this underground base."

Roger looked about the corridor and saw the activity mounting. "The invaders are craving their nighttime fix. It's gonna be a busy shift."

They became joined by several other guards who, unlike El-Te, were somewhat mechanical in movement.

Although tallish, thin, and human-looking, they had no facial expressions or emotions — like a Halloween mask. They were h-e-a-v-y breathing and seemingly genetically modified to look like a mixture of humans, metal elements, and electronic devices. They were "Humanoids" designed primarily to look like humans for intuitive collaboration. Their locomotor skills steadily improved to be on par with Homo sapiens movement. These Noids were known among human guards as "Noids," although they seldom talked to one another unless they had mind-to-mind telepathy.

When El-Te got near a Noid, he dropped his human facial expressions and feigned a face like them — no movement or emotion — to fit better with the Noids.

Dulce's underground was a multi-leveled complex with significant tunnelways and over three thousand cameras at various high-security locations throughout the spoke-wheeled complex. It expanded a mile in each direction before more appendages spread across much of the USA.

The group of humans and Noid guards went to Level 6, where advanced machinery abounded with sights and sounds:

The tip of an excellent drill.

A bolt of intense light.

A laser strobe is prepared to cut.

Circuits hissed and sparked near a human girl on a gurney, her feet squirming as the laser slowly moved up the legs fastened by clasps.

Along other corridors were genetic laboratories where freakish results of splicing human DNA to make horrible new hybrids. In different compartments, many kinds of animal crosses undertaken were beyond hideous-looking. Multi-legged 'humans' that looked half-human/half-octopus. There were also compartments of winged creatures, giants upwards of seven feet tall, and half-human, half-bird-like beings. In keeping with the nightmare show, reptilians and furry animals with hands like humans were crying like babies. Also in cages were mixtures of reptile-humans.

The Noids security group eventually came to a nearly football field-sized room; the closed door clicked open to allow them, Roger, El-Te, and other human guards to enter. They passed the first Holding Pen area containing young female/male adults aged six to twenty-two years, drugged and dazed, pleading for help.

Roger tried not to look at a female prisoner banging on the Plexiglas.

"Save us from these freaks!" she pleaded.

Though sympathetic toward her, Roger and El-Te continued with the Noid group to another —

As they bypassed her screams of panic, the Noids and others entered "Nightmare Hall." The hall had several large, barred, prison-like holding pens.

The door of Cell 33 clicked open, allowing the security team access. Young women in clinical robes scurried about on the edge of panic to avoid capture.

One disheveled but attractive woman in her late twenties with striking blue eyes and an upturned nose tripped within El-Te's reach. He whispered to her, "Do what we rehearsed...now."

The woman, Sally, got to her feet, staggering like a member of the living dead, lifting a seven-year-old disheveled but cherubic girl named Gina from the floor.

Sally shook the little one into pretend "play-acting." They begin staggering about in a stupor, bumping into other fleeing inmates, and finally, colliding with Carla Dawson, maneuvering to get out of their way.

El-Te caught up to Sally, gently holding onto this

woman who delighted his eyes. Roger took out a monitoring device, its needle poking her arm skin, extracting a drop of blood to monitor. The gauge didn't move.

El-Te did the same to little Gina, and the indicator remained still.

He released them; Sally and the little child staggered off in zombie mode.

Roger caught it all. "That pretty one, you gotta soft spot for her, huh?"

"Sally's spirit warms me like no other," El-Te admitted.

"Good, but these suckers don't care. We can't save Sally or 'er little friend."

El-Te became emotional. "I must. Let's get this over with."

They advanced upon a crowd of young women and girls huddling in a corner.

Noid sentries corralled another girl who screamed in sheer fright while trying to fight off her assailants. Roger pressed the device against her arm, needle pricking the skin. The dial spun wildly, clicking like a Geiger counter.

Roger and El-Te reluctantly dragged the girl away as a gamut of human emotions invaded them.

———

Hoses poured "blood" into oil drum containers at a nearby underground railway. A hydraulic lift run by Noid robot-like men set them onto a cargo train. When the flatbed became filled, the train disappeared through a tunnel.

———

At three-quarter level to the top of Mt. Archuleta—the Rock, Billy, with his German shepherd and Sam as a passenger, drove along an uninhabited road until parking deep in the bushes. When they were taking out supplies and setting up camp, the dog growled at the sight of a strange light blistering from the mesa into the sky until it disappeared.

Also heard were feint voices that sounded like radio transmissions interrupted by static and white noise.

"Voices often heard can't be understood, but they're there," Billy said. The dog growled towards the underground. "He knows it, too."

"Sometimes, weird things like this happen," the old Indian went on, "lights in the sky, different colors that vanish immediately. You think it may be an airplane, but that isn't the case. Their sky ships enter and leave cave openings in the cliff wall."

The bizarre occurrences brought out Sam's defiance directed to the sky. "If you bastards hurt my daughter, there's no black hole in the universe big enough for you to hide!" He directed his ire at Billy. "Get me inside!"

Billy took out a clay smoking pipe and lit the bowl, whose smell became suspicious to Sam—no doubt peyote from a small cactus plant mixed with herbs. "Pipe is a sacred ritual," he began. "Sometimes I smoke for relaxation, sometimes to talk to the spirit world."

Sam rolled his eyes in exasperation as Billy explained that the clay pipe represented the human's clay body, which contained the burning ember of life. As one smoked, the thoughts and prayers of the communicant went heavenward in the smoke.

Sam was beyond being impatient. "Time's running out, chief. Fast-forward to me."

––––––––––

Unbeknownst to Sam but prepared for it, in his room at the Gilmore Apartments, a black patrol van parked across the street, two Rock security men stepped out with a high-tech gadget to breach his room to search his belongings and whatnot.

War vet Sam and old Billy sat on the ground eating beef jerky, nuts, seeds, and fruit on the mesa, mindful of not making a fire to attract unwanted attention.

Sam received a buzz on his cell and checked it. "Rock men entered my apartment in town."

"I figured as much," Billy answered. "To understand Dulce, one doesn't look above your head but below your feet."

"Just get me inside!"

Eventually, the two odd fellows finished their snack meal. They studied the mountain roadways below where vehicles, lights on, were snaking up a mesa road.

Billy took out a pipe to smoke more peyote extract. "Jicarilla Apaches an' my Himmarshee tribe began in the underworld."

"Uh, Billy, I don't have time for a history lesson."

"Even if it could lead to your daughter?" Billy asked. "The same enemy you're facin' today forced us from our caves long ago."

The old Indian blew smoke and closed his eyes, and hallucinogenic images and altered perceptions began to appear to him. In his mind, he saw moving about in caverns an athletic-looking Indian youth with a bow in hand, leading a band of warriors.

Billy spoke aloud: "Nevazgane— the brave young warrior, with his mighty bow and help from Earth Mother and her children —the elk with mighty antlers, eagles with sharp talons followed by animals into a wide cavern. They shoot arrows at Sky People, who fire laser weapons in return. Nevazgane drove them away—back to the sky. Many warriors died, but Nevazgane had magic—arrowheads of flint— poison to the enemy invaders."

When Billy opened his eyes, the images disappeared.

He told more. "The Sky People went deeper in the cave to hide as Indians moved to live on the land, and the animals went back to the wild."

"Okay, Billy," Sam finally interrupted, getting up. "Sorry about all the crap your tribe went through, but how do I get in the fucking base?"

"Is my hearing goin' bad, or didya say you want answers?"

"You've been watching the Sci-Fi channel too much!"

"That so? I know why you couldn't kill that elk today."

"You might want to cut back on the peyote, chief!" Sam said with a lop-sided grin. "Whatever. I work best at night. See you in the morning."

He grabbed his bow and left like a phantom in the night.

CHAPTER 8

Sam climbed about the mesa as deftly as a mountain goat and traversed across a graveled road and vehicle lights below on the winding highway advancing toward him. The several vans snaking up the plateau turned off their lamps, and groups of armed men emerged near him, fanning out.

Sam's cell gave off another alert, a sound before he could shut it off. "Shit!" he mumbled to himself.

He realized a Rock surveillance man also heard it and gave a hand signal to the others who began making their way toward the noise. Sam scurried with a unique skill set, ending up at a dead-end cliff with a steep drop. The first Rock sentry cornered him where he had nowhere to run. Before the man could get off a shot, Sam spun into a flurry of punches and a kick that sent the guy toppling off the cliff, screaming, bouncing off the rock, and tumbling to death.

The shouts alerted other Rock men, now rushing towards the commotion. Although Sam's blood-lust was at a fevered pitch, he knew it best now to shift into survivor mode. Unlike the movies, combat soldiers didn't stand out in the open and calmly fire at the enemy. His primary concern was not to get hit when shot at. This defense had to do with a survival instinct. The combat was straightforward: first place and second place; second place was lying face down in the mud. Sam hung over the cliff by his fingertips, feet digging into tiny crevices for any support; one false move would send him to his death. *Carla.* Being pinned down had his survival instinct going full bore. He would not allow himself to end up dead on some rock pile.

As the Rock Men advanced, he heard one just above him using a flashlight beam to look below at the rock pile.

"It's McNeese!" the man said. "No fucking way to die!"

Just then came a rumbling sound of stampeding hooves advancing.

"What the?" the other man shouted.

An elk herd, a moving wall, converged on the two men who tried to move out of the way but became cornered at the cliff. A Rock security man fired at the herd, but an elk lunged loudly, vocalizing bugling screams, toppling the guy, the beast forcing the man over.

Sam heard their screams as they tumbled to their deaths. He worked his way atop the cliff, laying there gulping for air as a small herd of elks, their bodies compact and muscular, seemingly protecting him. "What's with you guys?" he asked the beasts. "Why are you following me?"

They continued nuzzling against him affectionately, wagging tails and licking his hands until eventually tromping off. And once again, they saved his life. But why? The herd crossing the roadside getting in the way of vans carrying gun-toting passengers? All that Sam thought was of his brief relationship with these Big Horn elk, attempting to take one down with an arrow, faltering.

Sam thought of the guy at the bar in Dulce, Roger. He was wrong about people trying to make Dulce into a *Twilight Zone*. It was spooky, pushing the lever to Sam's firing pin to its pressure point. War was about to be declared on the Dulce base.

Denver, Colorado

Late that night in the fashionable Capitol/Cheesman Park

neighborhood in the city's heart, Karen Dawson was home pouring over Websites about anything and everything about the Dulce Base in northern New Mexico—a box of Kleenex dwindling alongside her used ones in the nearby garbage.

Karen knew the Internet was a gold mine, but one needed to haul away tons of dirt to get to the gold. She realized Dulce base stories had been circulating for years. For everyone detailing the horrors of a capitulation of human leadership into a hell of compromises with off-world species interaction, another rumor debunked the whole subject; regardless of what was true and what wasn't, many articles detailed stories as ugly as possible.

Two hours later, after sifting through countless articles, Karen realized that the alleged secret alien-government underground Dulce base had several thousand Internet sites. She began pulling up reports from the *Center for Missing and Exploited Children*. Eventually, she settled her web search on children who had vanished in northern New Mexico near Dulce. A 1992 article in the *Albuquerque Journal* carried a report titled *N.M. High on the Missing Children List*.

It detailed New Mexico's disproportionate number of missing children compared to all other states in America. There were videos on the Web about these alleged abductees where they spoke about their time in these underground places and cities. The 1990s "milk carton" had kids ending up in these facilities, or so some speculated. Karen, thinking of the old saying, "Where there is smoke, there is fire," became ignited by the contact information of a medical husband and his outspoken wife on the Web. They hadn't given up searching the Dulce area for answers over their missing son and speaking out about the speculated atrocities at the base.

There was one name and contact of a person that intrigued her.

By early morning, Sam had returned to Billy's trailer home and saw him feeding his birds out back.

"How was huntin' last night?" the old Indian asked.

"Tell me more about Nevazgane."

Billy smiled. He drove Sam to his ranch to exchange into one of Harry Hatchet's cars to go by the Gilmore Apartments to try and get his belongings. A block away from the place, his cell rang.

"It's me," Karen said.

"Your call last night nearly got me killed."

"Try putting it on vibrating," she said. "You okay?"

"I'm fine. And no, I have yet to find Carla, but I must be getting closer. They sure don't want me around."

"There's a good reason. That's why I called."

Another Rock patrol van entered the motel lot. "Hold on."

Sam sank low in his parked car, shutting off the engine. Within moments, Roger appeared from one of the apartments to talk briefly with a Rock security guy before returning to his room. Two of these men entered Sam's room.

"The bull's eye on my back's getting larger," Sam whispered.

"Then lay low for a while," Karen advised. "I spoke to a couple in Albuquerque. You must go there to meet them."

"What? That's two hundred goddamn miles away!" Sam didn't want to hear it. "I'm not going anywhere. Carla could be —"

"Damn, you! Save her and listen!"

Sam made the two-hundred-mile ride to Albuquerque in one of Hatchet's cars, never once going past the speed limit, not wanting to be pulled over by the State Police boys. Following directions, he pulled into the driveway of an upper-middle-class stucco home in the high desert.

Opening the door was an erudite man in his sixties with a wild shock of white hair, extending his hand to shake. "Doctor Edward Stinson. Just call me Doc."

He checked the surroundings and didn't see anyone as he ushered Sam inside. "Don't be surprised if someone is watching us. It would help if you parked in front of the house next door. They won't mind."

Greeting Sam was Doc's wife, Judy, and Sam quickly realized that she was outspoken nobody's doormat. "I know what you're going through," she said. "Our son's been missing for six months."

"That's what my wife, er ex, Karen, said. How — ?"

Doc interrupted. "Nick was skiing along the New Mexico/Colorado border only a few miles from Dulce. Never seen again."

"What do they say happened?"

"An avalanche killed him," before Judy spat, "which is pure bullshit!"

"Calm down, hon."

"So you feel they abducted him?" Sam asked.

"We know so." Judy fought off tears.

"He was a brilliant skier," Doc added. "And there was no sign of an avalanche. We searched for months. I found others searching, too. Started sharing information. The Internet's full of stuff if you know where to look."

"To make matters more difficult for Archuleta Mesa to crack," Doc added, "it stands on an intrusion of tough augite andesite granite over three hundred feet thick. Some very sophisticated frequency analysis was done on the mesa, pointing out that whatever was under there put out energy of a city the size of New York."

He'd gone through the seismological catalogs for New Mexico. 1966 was hectic for the Archuleta Mesa region, with nine earthquakes located – 1.5 to 3.2 on the Richter scale. They all happened in late January to early February of that year. One earthquake had a 5.5-magnitude tremor.

"Was this a natural occurrence?" Doc asked rhetorically. "With the previous low earthquake activity in the area, some speculate Archuleta tremors became manufactured because of carving out the base. A couple of years later, an underground nuclear blast occurred about thirty miles southwest of Dulce, New Mexico, right off U.S. 64. This atomic blast was conducted under project Plowshare and was named Gassbuggy. Experts said it was to release natural gas reservoirs, but many feel that was hogwash, that the underground bases were undergoing expansion."

"Who controls Dulce?" Sam asked.

"Prepare yourself, Sam," Doc began. "You'll think we're crazy. Sometimes, I think we are. It perhaps began when some covert government agency made a treaty with a certain alien race years ago."

"For what purpose?"

Doc didn't hesitate. "The covert group wanted to acquire off-world antigravity technology, microchips, lasers, free energy, and more...the stuff we've all become addicted to. Now I can say with all certainty that's one of the main reasons the public stays in total darkness over Dulce. It's too close to home to do anything about."

"Who are these freaks below?" Sam asked.

"I'll tell lots more," Doc said, "but first, so I don't spook you over what's under our feet, another race is humanlike called *Hominids*. Peaceful, but they don't interfere with humanity."

"Good to know. Get back to the bad guys."

"The non-human looking are ruthless, violent, and destructive, craving something from us," Doc answered.

"We'll get to that soon," Judy added. "Think about it: how could a spokesman for the Pentagon dare admit that five or ten thousand feet underground exists an entire world that is foreign to a belief structure we have had for centuries?"

"How did this Dulce Base turn into a chamber of horrors?" Sam asked, perplexed.

Doc was well-versed in the goings on at the Jicarilla Indian Reservation. "Dulce is the new Area 51," he began. "But one story goes that back in 1954, under the Eisenhower administration, the federal government decided to bypass the Constitution of the United States and form a treaty with an off-world species."

"A treaty that stipulated what?" Sam asked.

"The off-world species signed a deal to give our government their advanced technology. In turn, they would be allowed to take a few cows and test their implanting techniques on a few human beings, but they have to give details about the people involved."

"Of course, the bastards lied," Judy added with a zing, "and they stopped abiding by the treaty." She pointed to photos of young adults posted on the wall with the caption "Missing Persons."

"This is the reason for all the secrecy," Doc explained. "If the public knew, they'd scream bloody murder. Hundreds of thousands of children and adults disappear annually in this country alone. Our government and media cover it by under-reporting the true numbers of those who disappear, often not reporting it at all, making it seem like they are just various cases of runaways or a spouse leaving with the children. Many people who vanish end up in these underground bases, never to be heard from again."

Judy nodded. "Hence the reason for all the secrecy at The Rock. If the public knew, they'd scream bloody murder."

Doc added, "Once you see this, you'll think that we have crossed over from the land of clear thinking concerning anomalous phenomena to the land of science fiction. Doc inserted a DVD into his television. A Dulce Base security officer named Tom Costello supposedly filmed this tape years ago without sound inside the base, which was now all over YouTube. After understanding the disturbing and inhumane projects at the base, he decided to escape with the evidence. Using a small camera, he also took 30 photos of locations within the multi-level complex."

The disc rolled, some of it sickening, bizarre experiments with humans: fusing humans with other animals, warped humans in different crossbreeding scenarios, others dead or suspended in a total body formaldehyde solution in a fluid tank. Security guard Costello had snapped several photos of multi-armed and multi-legged humans and hand-drawn diagrams. The unfathomable grotesqueness didn't stop there. Inside cages and vats were multi-legged creatures that looked half-human/half-octopus and aisles of furry animals with hands like humans and crying like babies. Fish, seals, birds, and mice could barely be considered those species.

Also, there was a photo of several expressionless and stiff-moving men.

"These are Humanoids," Doc went on. "Perhaps half-human, the other half wires, machinery, and whatnot."

"So they're making human prototypes?" Sam asked.

"It appears that way," but no more proof beyond these photos," Doc added. "That security man Costello spoke about the horrors on Level Six, which compelled him to flee the facility and made him feel as though he had to disclose what he knew to the public."

Doc went on, telling Costello that before hiding the original documents, he made five copies using "go-betweens" and distributed them to the UFO community. These documents became known as "The Dulce Papers" and were easy to find on the Internet. They contained what was said to be evidence that the underground base existed and provided insights into the terrifying experiments that have lived there for quite some time.

"Costello lived a life on the run until he went missing altogether," Doc added, "and so did his family."

"If my daughter…." Sam choked up.

"And our son," Doc said. "These sickos not of Earth don't care about our kids. As long as they get what they want."

"Which is?" asked Sam.

Doc answered. "One, they want to control our planet; another terrorizes our young before extracting blood from them."

"Why?"

"A fearful young person's endocrine glands secrete adrenaline into the bloodstream, the spiked blood called Adrenochrome, called "Adreno" for short."

Sam became irritated. "Speak English."

Doc broke it down. "The more fear inflicted on a young adult, the more intense the high for those drinking or injecting their adrenaline-rich blood. There's only one source for this stuff—the adrenaline glands from a living, preferably young, human body. It's no good if you get it out of a corpse."

Sam took on a sinking expression.

Judy added, "Many adult humans are addicted to the Adreno high. The spiked blood is a hot commodity, much more expensive than heroin or cocaine."

"Some sick stuff," Sam lamented. "Why isn't the government breaking up this evildoer ring?"

"Many dismiss this blood drinking as nothing more than an urban legend," Judy said, "an ancient practice or something only satanic cults do. They're so wrong."

Doc added, "Several journalists wanting to report on it were laughed out of their editors' offices."

The medical man rolled out a map. "The guard that managed to escape also made a map of the base's seven levels. He claimed the deeper you go, security increases. Someone built the Dulce Base on top of natural deep cavern honeycombs that extend hundreds of miles underground."

Sam's Special Forces instincts came alive as he studied the map. "I love maps. Anything's possible with the right one. But this won't be easy."

A fire rose inside Judy. "We'll fight for our son and no longer keep silent."

"We are at war," Doc added with intensity. "If humans don't stand up against this evil taking hold, they'll eradicate us. It's not if but when. Some off-world species is taking over our country, and when the veil becomes lifted, you'll see them increasingly baiting the human race as enslaved people in a planned New World Order ultimately to be controlled by them."

"Not if I can help it," soldier vet Sam Dawson voiced.

CHAPTER 9

Dulce Base, Level 6 – Nightmare Hall

Inside the mesa, the genetic labs were where crossbreeding experiments of humans and animals became the norm.

An incomprehensible Noid guard heard in his mind: *Bring us another.* He signaled some other Noids to enter Cell 33 to ignite the disheveled young women of different ethnicities in a panic, scurrying about to avoid seizure.

El-Te again became uncomfortable witnessing this. Possessed with an inner sense of right and wrong, the complex ethical and moral principles of what now took place were wreaking havoc on his mind. It had him making a dangerous decision when purposely bumping into the Noids while simultaneously dexterously pushing Sally away from their clutches. He then pointed to a livelier female for them to seize. They clutched onto the new one, the gauge against her arm spinning wildly. They dragged her away.

After the Noids made their quota of seizures, Sally dropped her catatonic posturing act, with Carla observing everything. "What did you just do?" Sally walked away, but Carla followed. "You faked being out of it. Why? How does it work?"

"Why should I tell you?" Sally asked. "So you can steal my survival tricks, get caught doing it, and blow my cover?"

"Yeah, thanks. You're just as heartless as they are! Where the hell am I?" She screamed in frustration and panic.

Sally grabbed her arm. "Here at Nightmare Hall, there

are two choices: learn how to stay alive another day or give up and be their guinea pig!"

"Oh God, what the hell am I in?"

Sally, sympathetic now, became less defensive. "What's it gonna be?"

"What can I do?"

"Learn all you can think about them," Sally insisted, "their schedule when they come in...sleep with one eye open, but above all, *hide your fear*."

"How?"

"To overcome fear," Sally answered, "El-Te coaxes me to breathe deeply, let it pass by. In other words, work on yourself. Do as much as possible to become what a human intended to become. In a way, the positive energy force I create will help me fight them off, feeding on my life forces where it is difficult to walk because their feed process leaves me in a weakened and lethargic condition. Sometimes, they zero in on the heart area to the point of causing it to race so fast that it feels as if it is going to burst."

"What's that thing they put on your arm?"

"Human fear produces hormones which the Controllers feed off of getting high. It's like Crack for them."

"Controllers? The weirdo Creatures?"

"No," Sally explained. "Some believe Controllers are off-world aliens controlling these Noid freaks, and the human guards call 'Noids.' That gizmo they put on our arms measures our fear count. If high, that means adrenaline is pumping through our body. Noids have an insatiable appetite for biological enzymes, hormonal secretions, and blood."

"I'm so scared. If those freaks read my high fear—"

"I've learned to control mine," Sally said. "So I've been passed over for someone else. But there's something we can't hide....our menstruation."

"What?"

"Right after, it is prime time for their little experiments."

"Oh, God," Carla realized, "I'm bleeding now!"

"When you're ripe, they'll know, for they can detect its metallic copper smell. Clean yourself often."

"So whoever gets taken inside gets it one way or another?"

"Depends on the mood they're in."

"Where are these Noids from?"

"From what I've heard from human guard talk," Sally answered, "Noids are a manufactured mix of flesh and blood human and mechanical and electrical parts. They do the dirty work while those who control stay concealed below Level Seven."

"This is sick! Before I saw someone helping you, clearly not a Noid, so humanlike, but—"

"He's...I don't know what El-Te is," Sally admitted. "A mix for sure, but mostly human, his emotions intact. He's become my guardian angel, trying to help me through this, at least for another day. Taught me to control my fear."

"Why is El-Te helping you?"

"He feels sorry for us, but with me..."

Little Gina giggled. "El-Te and Sally like each other and sneak kisses."

Sally motioned Carla to a lone corner in the cell block. "Let's talk over here."

Sam's daughter soon learned that little girl Gina's mother had been dragged away a month ago by the Noids, never to return. Gina felt her mother would rely heavily on Sally's emotions. Carla went with her, glad to have a friend.

———————

Albuquerque

At Doc's home, Sam's foul mood continued. "Dulce base is a goddamn heinous crime against humanity!" he shouted. "Why aren't government law authorities cracking down on this?"

Judy answered, "The whistleblower guard we mentioned escaping Dulce's underground base more than suspected something very diabolical happening there. He drew a detailed map of its seven levels leading to the nightmare."

Doc added, "We must use that escaped security guard's map of the base to help fight for our son, not stay silent."

Sam clenched a fist. "I'm in!"

"Okay," Doc said, "but also first hear about another fear, what happened to another brave man."

"Go on."

"A geologist, Phil Schneider, who helped build Dulce and other underground bases, began lecturing publically about the nightmares below Dulce's Level 7. A conscious man with high-security clearance, Schneider knew that if he kept talking, he'd become a marked man."

"And he didn't stop talking, so they did him in?"

"It appears so," Doc answered.

From his computer, he brought up a segment of Schneider speaking. "Listen to some of his last lectures two months before his murder. It's most astonishing and yet somehow seems completely matter-of-fact. He doesn't seem at all like a man that's lying."

The screen began playing, and a burly, simple-speaking man in his fifties with white hair was at the podium addressing a large crowd in a banquet hall. "...Much of what I'm going to say will be very shocking, totally unbelievable, so, instead of putting your glasses on, I'm asking you to put your 'skepticals' on. But please, feel free to do your homework. I know the Freedom of Information Act isn't much to go on, but it's our best. The local law library is an excellent place to look for Congressional Records. So, if one continues to do their homework, one can stand vigilant regarding their country.

"I love the country I'm living in more than I love my life," said Schneider assuredly, "but I wouldn't be standing before you now, risking my life, if I didn't believe it was so. The first part of this talk will concern deep underground military bases and the black budget. The Black Budget is a secretive budget that garners twenty-five percent of the gross national product of the United States. The Black Budget currently consumes one point twenty-five trillion dollars per year. Some used least that amount in black programs like those concerned with Deep Underground Military Bases called DUMBs. Presently, one-hundred and twenty-nine of these DUMB bases are in the United States, growing yearly."

Sam's laser-like eyes studied the computer screen, taking in Schneider's Intel and realizing that these underground military bases were so sensitive that they were exempt from standard reporting requirements to Congress.

"Back in 1979," Phil Schneider continued, "a firefight at Dulce occurred by accident. I was involved in building an addition to Dulce's underground military base, a DUMB base that goes very deep. It goes down seven levels and is over two-and-a-half miles deep. At that particular time, we had drilled four distinct holes in the desert, and we would link them together and blow out large sections at a time."

Schneider continued. "My job was to go down the holes, check the rock samples, and recommend the explosive to deal with the particular rock. We found ourselves amidst a large cavern full of off-world species as I headed down there. I shot two of them. At that time, there were thirty people down there with me. About forty more came down after this started, and they all got killed. We had surprised a whole underground base of existing aliens. Anyway, I got shot in the chest with one of their weapons, a box on their body that blew a hole in me and gave me a nasty dose of cobalt radiation. I've had cancer because of that."

Schneider lifted a hand to show his audience that he had lost several fingers during the firefight and revealed his chest scar.

Doc moved forward to another Schneider segment when the geologist said, "Now, I'm angry about the federal government's activity. They have lied to the public, stonewalled senators, and refused to tell the truth regarding non-human species matters."

Schneider said with sadness that the democracy he loved no longer existed: we had become a technocracy ruled by a shadow government intent on imposing their view of things on us, whether we like it or not.

Sam listened in rapt to Schneider's twenty-five-minute speech. Towards its end, Schneider's words became eerily accurate.

"If I keep speaking out like I am, maybe God will give me the life to talk my head off. I'll break every law that it takes to talk my head off. Eleven of my best friends in the last twenty-two years became murdered, eight of them called suicides."

Doc turned off the computer. "Schneider gave many speeches like this with much more information. I believe him."

"An underground war with aliens?" Sam asked skeptically. "Very strange, Intel."

Doc agreed. "After someone murdered Schneider, other military and scientific personnel feeling the need to speak out did so anonymously. They said that after the battle, the otherworld ones left Dulce for a while, only to regroup to return to start another breeding program but with lower numbers."

Doc continued with his extreme knowledge of the Dulce Base. "Schneider braved the chance to alert people on the horrors at Dulce, real dark stuff that the government wasn't disclosing. He knew he was a marked man and didn't expect to live long. Shortly after his last lecture, Schneider became assassinated, strangled with a piano wire around his neck in an execution-style murder."

Sam didn't flinch. "Danger doesn't faze me; it has always been a part of my soldiering. I want my daughter. Give me that map to figure out how to get into underground Dulce."

The ex-war vet told the couple about Major Briggs, who he speculated to be working with the military on DUMB bases. "He warned me about people after me. I know he wants to confess more, but maybe he doesn't want to end up like this guy Schneider."

"I can understand that," Doc answered, "but there's a good chance they transmit voice into his brain or the inner ear. He could also hear music, knocking on the door, and other sounds when nobody was there. The off-world ones can make a person look either schizophrenic or paranoid."

Doc and Judy named several other informants who'd become too loose with their knowledge of what was going down at Dulce. Some became discredited in many ways, and others — a couple of thousand of them had unfortunate accidents or disappeared.

The kitchen phone rang. Judy returned to Sam. "It's your wife, ah, ex."

Sam went to the corner of the living room for privacy to talk to his ex-wife.

"Hey," he said, "I made it here. Glad I did."

"Talk to me, Sam," Karen said, her voice choking. "I can't take this anymore. An investigator can—"

"No! Listen to me only. Cool heads prevail. I'll save Carla, wherever she is, or die trying."

"I need to be there!"

"You will, but not yet," Sam insisted. "Nothing can be allowed to tip off the enemy."

"If the Dulce Base is for real, how do you fight aliens?"

"I'm working on it," Sam assured. "Be ultra-careful in communicating; don't tip anyone off what's happening, and don't use your regular phone or email. Talk later."

"Sam, be cautious. I'll pray for you from—"

"Head to toe."

"Yes. How many times have I said that to you?"

"A lot over the years."

"I'm not done yet."

"That's good to know."

A black van just parked across the street, near Sam's car. Doc looked out his window. Two dark-suited men got out. "Our usual company's checking in on us."

Judy swung into action. "I'll keep them busy while you boys do your thing. We could use some ice cream anyway. Chocolate chip, okay?"

She went for her coat and car keys as Doc opened the door to the garage. "Follow me."

He led Sam to the back of the garage. As Judy got into her car, they went through another door into the backyard; right before the door opened, Judy drove out in a tinted-window vehicle down the street, the black van following.

In Doc's backyard, he led Sam into the garage of the house next door. It was only a few feet away, with no fence between the properties, and they were hidden from the street by a wooden wall stretched between the two garages. They entered the other garage interior, and Doc turned on a small overhead light. There was a Jeep Cherokee with a U-Haul attached.

"When our neighbors retired," Doc explained, "we bought their place as an investment for Nick."

Doc took Sam inside the house to a small medical lab. He opened a drawer to display a microchip. "Several brave men — desperate parents, husbands, and wives, lost their lives for what I'm about to show you. It's alien technology. Part of what we get is for giving them a home. When some peoples' headaches and nightmares wouldn't go away, a brain scan revealed these. Surgeons removed these chips from abducted people and then released them. The guard who escaped also had one."

He explained microchips were attached to major nerve centers, primarily through the nasal passage to the brain. Tissues would grow in and around them, making the implant a part of the nervous system. When that growth occurred, relatively unsophisticated medical procedures to remove the implants could damage the nerve centers. As a result, it could cause severe injury. It was highly meticulous work.

"What's its purpose?"

"We're not sure, but it enables the aliens to communicate by thought."

"Telepathy?"

"Yes," Doc answered. "And the unlucky ones are being implanted with brain transceivers. These act as telepathic communication "channels" and telemetric brain manipulation devices. In essence, the off-world ones control the person implanted. It means someone could be controlling everyone at Dulce and will be against us."

Sam's military mind was humming. "We could use

some backup. You have a secure line?"

Doc handed him the landline on the wall. "Try this."

Sam dialed a number. "Brock...*Sine pari!*"

A powerful voice returned the slogan, "*Sine pari!*"

"I could use your bas-ass ways to help penetrate a maximum security target."

"Abso-fucking-lutely! Never Say Never!" Brock said, full of excitement. "Got a meeting now that I need to wrap up quickly."

"You'll need to gather up a few supplies. And don't show up too conspicuous.

———

A shirtless Brock terminated the call in an athletic locker room, wearing boxing trunks and small open-finger gloves pads. His blocky build was the perfect core frame for a world-class performance athlete, as was his six feet and two-hundred and thirty-five-pound gladiator physique with only five percent body fat. He left the locker room to enter a steel cage ring.

At the opening bell, Brock came out like a hulked-out 'roid-enraged beast, seemingly with his hair on fire. He unleashed a flurry of jabs and kicked the challenger's torso and head until he got the even larger opponent on the mat. Brock performed a couple of power moves until he gave his "finisher" signature move—python-like thick arms squeezing the bloody-faced opponent until a bone cracked, and then another.

CHAPTER 10

Dulce Military Base

At Level 7, Roger and El-Te moved along a long corridor filled with cavern-like rooms containing artificial underground farms from hybridized seed stocks nourished by ultraviolet light. The base provided water from a re-directed small underground river, making edible nourishment for the captives.

Roger suddenly realized how deep into the base they were. "I don't have Ultra Seven clearance to be here! If caught, I sure don't wanna be the queen's lunch! What's her name again?"

"Lamia."

El-Te cocked his head, picking up something beyond the normal five senses. "We have eight minutes and thirty-five seconds before someone could detect us. Quick, this will only take a minute. I want to show you what I've never shared with anyone."

He led Roger into another corridor filled with row upon row of thousands of humans, including some children in various stages of development, in cold storage or floating in a peach-colored broth solution in storage vats. El-Te stopped before one, his face filling with wonder, mesmerized by a naked dead woman, perhaps thirty, afloat as if in a cloud, beautifully preserved. Her face, seemingly made of white marble, appeared very young, more like a youthful maiden than a grown woman. Her slightly smiling lips were finely curved, and her eyes large with an enchanting look, seemingly falling into eternity without return. Her long hair floated in the solution like sea foam; her open eyes changed from a light blue to green. The whole effect had her appearing as a sea goddess.

"She's beautiful." Roger became mesmerized by her loveliness. "How do you know she's the one?"

"My human side has always suspected her of being my mother," El-Te said, "my Raker side knows for certain."

Roger looked about at the endless rows of dead people. "Why do Rakers do this slaughtering of people?"

"They're a dying species needing to save themselves," El-Te answered. "Their planet has no resources left. Earth has certain minerals they need, especially gold and magnetic force, that provide the power source they need. They also want human energy and souls because they don't have them in their makeup. They're working on a plan to colonize here. In the meantime, humans also provide them with nourishment."

"The vats with the gooey red broth—their Breakfast of Champions?" Roger asked.

"Sorry to say yes."

They retraced their steps. At the other end of the corridor, a massively thick vaulted metal door gave off an odd pulsating life force.

"What's that about?" Roger asked.

"Below Level 7, strictly off limits."

"What's down there?"

"Raker headquarters, tentacles of underground webbing throughout the planet. Rakers don't fear humankind, which they feel they can easily conquer. Much of America is honeycombed with naturally occurring caves and cave systems, sinkholes, and abandoned mines, especially in the western states."

A buzz went off on El-Te's waistband device. "Let's get to lunch in time. Hurry!"

They ran out of the area to avoid detection.

El-Te and Roger arrived at the eating area to split off, Roger following other human workers to eat sandwiches and fruit. El-Te and the Noids veered off to go to their infamous feeding vats. These ten-foot wide containers look like a child's portable swimming pool lined with copper, the exterior walls clad with stainless steel. Afterward, they used a spoon to drink a distilled concoction made into a high-protein broth. A high-tech mechanical arm made of a copper alloy stirred the amber broth, comprised of bovine blood, body parts, and human features, generally glands. The stirring devices stopped the blood from coagulating. Since most Noids possessed weak digestive systems, they rolled up their sleeves and used sponges to smear the soupy mixtures onto their bodies, absorbing nutrients into their skins.

From a distance, Roger observed the ritual that El-Te detested — sponging with blood and drinking some of the foul mixture concoction. Roger heard the humming sound of the vat arm and smelled its pungent formaldehyde. He couldn't finish his sandwich when El-Te became forced to rub the horrific blend onto his body and taste some fake being a trusted Noid so they wouldn't report him and possibly get him killed.

Roger noticed a Noid observing an expressionless El-Te drinking the blood subtly, spitting it out before dipping for more. Aware that a Noid alongside was suspicious of him, El-Te made sure the Noid saw him rubbing the blood mixture on his body and swallowing a mouthful. No longer wary of El-Te, the Noid returned to slurping while El-Te eventually left for the lavatory to throw up furtively.

Albuquerque

Judy, Doc, and Sam were in the garage dressed to leave. Judy got in her car. Doc kissed her through the open window. "It won't be long now. Love you, hon."

"Same here, you old coot. Be careful."

"Just be ready with everything when I send you the Go signal."

As predicted, Judy's car again pulled out of the garage, down the driveway, and into the street, the black patrol van following.

Next door, Doc's Jeep with U-Haul pulled out of the garage and down the driveway. Sam exited the garage to get in his car parked on the street. They drove off in the opposite direction from Judy and the black van.

Judy looked in the rear-view mirror to see they'd take the bait and floored the gas pedal. "C'mon, you knuckleheads," she spat. "Let's see if you can peel rubber!"

She tore around several corners to an open stretch of the road far away from Doc and Sam's route. She pulled into a mini-mall to an ice cream shop, the car following screeching to slow down before slowly passing, she throwing them the middle finger.

Sam drove alone back to Dulce, followed by thoughts of his combat days filled with harrowing missions. Where Sam was now about to venture was going against an unknown enemy with supposed off-the-chart intelligence controlling his daughter, or worse. All attacks are well thought out, knowing the enemy like the back of their hands beforehand.

Just thinking of Carla's peril had Sam gripping the steering wheel so hard that it was on the verge of snapping. If they had harmed her, Sam knew he'd become a kamikaze soldier if he found the key to barge into the Dulce base to kill as many enemies as possible before they killed him.

——————

Three hours later, Sam hid in bushes alongside a sign that read "Dulce City Limits."

An Ice Cream truck drove along the highway toward Sam, the truck's logo reading *Freddy the Frozen Custard — We're a Real Softie*. The vehicle slowed at the city limit sign, allowing Sam to jump inside only to conceal himself quickly. While he did, he became overcome with laughter over Brock's ice cream vendor get-up! Brock was adorned in a fat suit, faux tattoos—hippie peace signs and flower child types—puca shell necklace, and a long-haired wig. "Looks like fatso ate his entire product!"

"Fucking-A-Funny, man," Brock said before joining in the laughter.

"Keep it on until we're in the clear. Thanks for coming, bro."

"Hey, old Special Forces warriors never die. You need me; I'm fuckin' here."

"Even if it means going against our government?"

"If someone's breaking the Constitution they swore to uphold, fuck 'em! Got some presents for them, too!"

Sam knew well this guy's bravado was no act. He was a true American badass. Often tested in life-and-death situations, Brock had no fear valve. And on top of having nerves of steel, he was utterly gonzo! This formidable ex-Special Forces badass didn't flinch at the frightening sound of missiles exploding around him. This wall of granite protected the soldier unit that he loved. Those he didn't like had better kill him or head for the hills if they blotched an attempt.

Sam looked for space to put his bag. He found a spot behind the dairy equipment where he saw an arsenal of automatic rifles, explosives, and other dangerous-looking supplies. Brock tossed Sam a new cell phone. "Catch."

The Ice Cream truck on Harry Hatchet's ranch passed his simple home and moved a cavern Archuleta Mesa to a small log cabin at the base of bounders and a small mesa. Hatchet saw them and got in his car to drive alongside Brock's truck to join Sam in laughter, watching Brock take off his "fat suit" of blubber to reveal his true muscular and badass self.

Hatchet looked inside the truck. "Starting World War Three, are we?"

"If we have to," Brock answered.

"Feels good to be back on a mission," Hatchet said.

"Not good, fucking outstanding!" Brock exclaimed.

"Over here." Hatchet guided them to the boulders, leading to a small mesa. Rocks and shrubbery were at the base, concealing an opening. A creature termed a "cabbit" had the head and shoulders of a cat, and the body of a rabbit with long ears, while its voice was half growl, half meow was there and hopped away.

"That's weird."

"Na. You wanna see weird?" Hatchet asked. They followed him nearby, where a horrifically mutilated cow lay behind a boulder.

"Someone has a nasty diet," Brock said.

"They're 'mutes'...mutilations," Hatchet explained. "Common around here. Some say over ten thousand since 1980, and no one ever charged with a crime."

Sam scrutinized the slaughtered cow before them. "Killed in a very precision surgical way...mutilated but no blood...anus, eyes, genitals, and rectum removed. No wild animal did this." He pointed to a section of the cow. "These precision cuts...the edges of the wound appear seared, leaving a hard, smooth edge along the cut lines. They also took out the tongue, and the surrounding ground appears to have been heated or burned. The work of a powerful laser."

"An' there haven't been no flies landing on the carcass, no coyotes touching it either," Hatchet added. "This can lie in the sun for weeks and never be touched by flies or coyotes."

Hatchet motioned them over toward the cavern. "Help me with this."

They dismantled the rock pile, setting them aside and some shrubbery, thus allowing them to drive their vehicles into the cave. They rolled away several faux boulders and shrubbery, setting them aside and allowing them to move their cars into the shelter. The shafting light from the outside displayed startlingly deep chasms, unseen passages, and trickling waterways. Adding to the beauty were stalactites hanging from the ceiling and stalagmites rising from the floor. Some even met to create a column. Other formations looked like needles, popcorn, pearls, and flowers, while others of the cavern contained massive, sharp figures of minerals.

"The mother of all caves!" Brock said in awe.

"How far does it go?" Sam wanted to know.

"Miles in every direction...deep too." Hatchet lit lanterns and guided them through the labyrinthine passageways with high ceilings. "Always cool, with good ventilation. No elements to deal with, no nagging wives!"

"Home, Sweet Home," Brock said with glee.

A makeshift table became set up for food as the three former soldiers and Billy ate with gusto.

"Tell the weaknesses of those controlling the base?" Sam asked.

"Flint arrowheads, for one," old Billy answered quickly. "Poisons 'em like a rattler bite."

Brock held up his automatic. "This works faster."

Hatchet dragged over a large duffel bag, opening it to

unveil many flint arrows and knives.

"You've killed them with these things?" Sam asked.

"Nope."

"Just more Indian folklore?"

"Mebbe more than that."

"Folklore? Is that our fucking Intel?" Brock asked with a snort.

"Whatever might work, we bring," leader Sam answered.

"Also, don't let them sense your fear," Hatchet added. "They feed off of it."

"Break that down for me," Brock wanted to know.

"They read our emotions," Hatchet believed. "They have some power to tap into other people's thoughts and actions. They can smell when someone's afraid or lying, all sorts of shit."

"So? We got animals that can smell 'em out!" Old Billy didn't become fazed.

"What's he talking about now?" Brock asked.

As Billy merely smiled, Sam took out his bottle of constipation relief pills and popped one.

———

A darkened sky illuminated by stars and peaceful looking was the backdrop to a Jeep with a U-Haul pulling up to Lone Wolf's ranch. Smoking a pipe nearby, Billy made an Indian bird howl to signal Hatchet, who came out of the cave with Sam.

"You made it, Doc," Sam said in greeting. "Great!"

Old Billy sized up the Medicine man. "Are you a warrior, too?"

"No, sir. Just a fool ready to fight to get my son back."

"I hear ya," Billy said.

"This way," Hatchet directed. "Hurry!"

He guided Doc's Jeep and U-Haul into the cavern. The U-Haul contents became unloaded as assorted gadgetry, and a CAT scanning machine spread about the cave. As soon as it was in, Hatchet's son rode their dirt bikes over the tire marks, erasing them and kicking up dust.

Doc got the group up to speed on their research as they set up the equipment.

CHAPTER 11

Dulce, Nightmare Hall- Cell 33

Carla was with Sally, who'd just fallen asleep. She was about to do the same before noticing the young man in the adjacent pen gazing at her with a languid grin still carrying a unique magnetism.

Sam Dawson's daughter slid over to him. Unable to hear one another due to the partition, they continued mouthing communication. "Thanks for helping me."

He shrugged and mimicked the words, "We all have to look out for each other…can't give up hope."

Carla also used the same communication. "How long have you been here?"

"Three months, maybe four. I've lost track of time."

"Three days for me," Carla communicated.

"I haven't seen you. You're easy on the eyes, a welcome relief from this nightmare."

Carla thought about his comment before asking, "Have they hurt you?"

"No," Nick answered, gesturing to his groin area. "I'm rich in sperm." His hands then made a gesture of a woman with a bulge at her stomach. "They use me to impregnate women."

"Why?"

"They take out the fetus at three months to put into an alien female."

"This is sick!" Carla mouthed.

The young man nodded. "Tell me about it." Pause. "I want to help you."

"How?"

"I don't know, but I will," Nick got across.

She swallowed a lump in her throat and tapped her breast, mouthing, "I'm Carla."

"Nick," he communicated with a beautiful, wholesome smile. He flattened the palm of his hand against the Plexiglas. Carla hesitated until her instincts had her placing hers against his. Though the barrier prevented them from touching, it could not block out the warmth between them.

Later in the day, El-Te returned to Cell 33 to catch another glimpse at his love, Sally, and try to tell him more about himself, which his sixth sense picked up.

El-Te began mopping the floor near her, not looking at her, and spoke in hushed tones. "I know you have many questions about my physical makeup if we can be compatible."

"Yes, I do, El. Quite a few."

"Okay, I'll need to say this quick before anyone detects us talking," El-Te said. "Although my rare humanoid type is externally almost identical to humans, there are subtle differences in physiology. I have a larger lung capacity than humans and copper-based blood to carry oxygen more efficiently. My eyes are protected by inner lids, allowing them to see into the ultraviolet range of the spectrum. My heart is lower in my chest than a human heart. I have no sweat glands. My heartbeats are around two hundred and forty beats a minute, which is typical. Average blood pressure is eighty systolic and forty diastolic. My urine is thick with minerals and appears in color and texture like freshly squeezed orange juice. Feces extraction is once a day — small, dry pellets with all moisture removed.

"Whereas Raker females are capable of being impregnated at any time, but the males are capable of impregnation about once a year; thus the reason why human male sperm is something Rakers vigorously goes after."

Sally suppressed a snicker. "Whoa, too much for me to comprehend at one time."

"Of course, sorry. Let me end with a big question I sense you want to know: how will lovemaking be for us?"

"Uh, yeah," she hesitated. "What size? Ah, well, you know."

El-Te got to the point. "My penis is the same look and size as a human male, perhaps slightly larger by an inch or two. You and I are physically attracted to one another, and I have healthy human sperm. So I look forward to us making love someday. And often."

"What is 'often' to you?"

El-Te's longing smile at her was interrupted when two Noid security men entering the cell had El-Te and Carla moving away from each other.

_____

Hatchet Cave

Once the CAT scanner received electricity to make it operable, Doc asked the motley crew of men.

"If an implant corrupts someone, it can manipulate and control people. This CAT scan will detect it. Often, these chips can read your thoughts, hear what you are saying, and even see what you see, depending on the chip, like a video. You know the rule: trust but verify."

"Okay, guys," Sam said. "I'll go first. But you know, Doc, we three ex-soldiers got a shitload of war metal inside us."

He passed through the scanner that detected his

defibrillator.

Brock was next to be scanned, and the machines detected various metal objects.

"Son, what's inside you?" Doc asked.

"Souvenirs. That large piece of metal in my ass is from Desert Storm with Love! An' the one in the shoulder, would you believe I was drunk and wrestling with a big-boned gal in bed, and we fell out? She fell on top of me hard. It messed up my shoulder. Two pins in there."

Billy was cleaning his smoking pipe on the porch with a long knife the following morning when he noticed several eagles soaring above, squawking ferociously. He gave a howling call, and one returned from inside the cavern.

A black government Rock van pulled up, and two Archuleta men got out before Billy.

"A convict broke out of prison...white guy," the Rock man made known, showing him a photo of Sam Dawson. "Did you see this guy?"

"Nope. The only thing I see is your palefaces!" Billy quipped deadpan. "Get some sun! I hear Miami's nice this time of year."

"We need to look around," the other Rock security man alerted.

"Good. Don't want no lawbreakers disturbin' the peace 'round here."

As the men looked about, Billy noticed holsters inside their jackets.

Through a crack in the boulders, Hatchet saw the Rock men casing the area, looking over the countryside, finding nothing unusual until they noticed a flock of eagles above.

"What's with them?" one asked Billy.

"They're watchin' buzzards. Somethin' must have died up on Archuleta. Mebbe, your convict is their lunch."

The Rock men got back in their van and drove off.

_____

Dulce Base

El-Te and Roger were inside a storage room, putting away their cleaning items. The half-human filled a scrub bucket with water.

"Are we done for the day?" Roger asked. "Need to go to a bar after today's bloodbath."

"Be careful."

"You're not the same ever since meetin' Sally."

"She gives me a reason to live," Ed-Te admitted. "I never had that before."

"El, you've been bitten by the love bug!"

The Hubrid-3 shrugged. "Analytically, I understand nature's beautiful way of keeping the human species alive and reproducing. Your scientists say deciding if you're falling for someone takes ninety seconds to four minutes. With Sally, I knew in five seconds."

"Good for you, Einstein," Roger said, scrubbing his hands. "Hope you don't move that fast if you ever get to make love with Sally!"

El-Te cocked his head, giving an unusual smile. "Your sense of humor...odd but amusing. I understand that the sex hormones testosterone and estrogen drive the first stage of love. That amazing time when one is truly love-struck and unable to think of anything else."

"That's you!" Roger chuckled. "Sally has your head spinning."

"Yes, my adrenaline, dopamine, and serotonin neurotransmitters are disrupted. When I'm near here, my cortisol also rises. I begin to sweat, my heart—"

"Races, the mouth goes dry?"

"Yes. How—"

"The same thing happened to me when I fell in love with my wife."

"Good for you, Roger. My affection for Sally is now an addiction. Looking at her beautiful face and feeling the goodness of her heart, I see she's beginning to change how I think. What would it be like for us to live on the surface of Earth? I've never seen it."

"Sorry, buddy, but Sally's chances of making it outta here ain't good."

"That's why I am making a plan."

———

El-Te entered his favorite place in life, cellblock 33, cleaning an area of the floor with a scrub bucket and mop. He glanced at Sally off in a corner with Carla— napping on a cot, inching over to them.

He moved to Sally, whispering. "Have Carla wash away menstrual blood before the Noids detect it."

He slid over the bucket.

"I love you," Sally whispered.

El-Te smiled and drifted off to mop in another direction to avoid detection.

Sally nudged Carla and murmured directions to her. Her back to the corridor and cameras, Carla faced the holding pen adjacent to hers. She opened her gown, sponge-washing the groin area.

Peering from the other pen was a boyishly handsome twenty-year-old, Nick, gazing at Carla through tired eyes. He gave a hand signal of apology for her private matter and looked away.

Carla washed away her period blood from her privates after ensuring no enemy was looking.

Nick motioned for her to dispose of the tainted bucket

of water, and Carla emptied it into the drain. Making her way back to Sally, she glanced at the handsome youth who flashed a weak smile.

———————

Sam drove with Brock in Hatchet's truck through the countryside, concealed in Indian attire but on the lookout for something.

"Armageddon! That was okay, Brock said, "but aliens…? Ooh, that is f-u-c-k-e-d up."

"So what's your point, Tonto?" Hatchet asked.

"Just weighing my chances," Brock said. "I keep thinkin' of that mutilated cow."

———————

Deep in the bowels of Rock Mountain in Dulce's Level 6 Nightmare Hall, the screaming abounded as another holding pen raid in Cell 33 was in progress. Inmates hurried to the far corners of one while Sally, going into a faux comatose mode, had the Noids bypassing her.

Imitating Sally, Carla didn't run this time and had worked to make herself look unappealing while feigning a zombie-like demeanor. An aggressive Noid grabbed her and put the reading device against her arm. The needle barely moved. The work in progress Noid pushed her aside, and the frenzy continued as he stalked one of the livelier-looking girls. Carla collapsed to the floor in relief.

Carla and Sally, again off alone, spoke in hushed tones.

"You got someone on the outside?" Sally asked.

"My Dad. He'll find us."

"I don't think anyone can find us down here."

"You don't know my dad."

As the two women slumped on the floor in a corner, the emotions of the raid sapping their energy, Carla thought of her dad. Never was he home much when she was a little girl but deployed in some country fighting the enemy in another war that harmed Americans or their allies. However, when Sam came home on leave for a week or two here and there, they were inseparable. And how could she forget the day she was in the fourth grade and he made a surprise visit to the school assembly in uniform? She could not stop crying when he located her in the crowd and hugged and hugged her before he spoke to the children about how American soldiers were protecting children like them from harm's way.

Carla looked about the holding pen at so many teens contained like animals, some perhaps twelve and thirteen years old. And Carla realized she was in the same boat as them, no doubt destined to be alien food, some heinous experiment, or for breeding. Most assuredly, the parents would never hear from them again, nor would they get to hug their parents.

Carla thought again of her father hugging her in school with his entire mind, whispering in her ear, "No matter where I am or where you are, I'll always be with you." She laid her head on the floor sobbing uncontrollably, wishing those words were actual.

———————

Dulce Base Laboratory – Level 5

Nick lay atop a gurney table.

Two human surgeons, seemingly mind controlled with no emotions, worked on attaching his penis inside a flexible tube. A machine's vibrating movements aroused Nick into ejaculation, his semen caught in the receptacle.

"We need more semen," the surgeon notified the youth.

"I'm drained and need time to recuperate," Nick answered. "Need time to build up more."

"No time."

Another Noid pushed an attractive half-naked girl of

seventeen, whimpering in fright inside the room.

"Sorry you have to do this," Nick said soothingly. "Get it over with."

"What do you mean?"

"Help me ejaculate. I hope it works. If not—"

The girl looked away while fondling Nick's genitals. However, he wasn't getting aroused enough to climax.

"Use your mouth instead of hands," the surgeon ordered the girl.

Several Noids formed an intimidating circle around her.

"If you want to live, do it," Nick offered.

The Noids pushed the distressed girl's face to Nick's penis, forcing her to perform oral sex.

Nick became aroused, signals that he was on the verge of ejaculating.

These creatures pushed aside the humiliated girl so Nick's precious sperm could be collected.

Carla thought more of Father Sam. He was never home much when she was a child but deployed in a foreign country fighting the enemy in another war that harmed Americans or their allies. However, when he came home on leave, the two were inseparable even though this highly trained warrior was viewed as an unstoppable force worldwide, taking on bad guys and getting themselves out of impossible situations. Most thought they were a group of guys who blew a lot of stuff up.

Sam informed the children that the Special Forces Latin motto, "De Oppressor Liber," basically translated to "To free the oppressed." These soldiers endured great hardship to become an elite fighting force protecting the United States from threats worldwide.

"Are you a real-life superhero character?" a child student asked innocently.

"No, I can't fly and don't have superpowers," Sam answered with a chuckle. "All I do is work to keep America safe from anyone trying to hurt our great country."

Carla broke from her reverie, wondering if Special Forces soldiers protected America from threats worldwide. Did that include "under" the world? She looked at various teens held like animals, perhaps twelve years old. She felt they would never be heard from again, never getting to hug their parents. Carla realized she was in the same boat as them, destined to be alien fodder for some heinous Frankenstein experiment or breeding. She shook away thoughts of her body mutilated, flayed, and dismembered and stacked upon the other lifeless, like cords of wood.

She thought again of her father coming to her school, them hugging and him whispering in her ear, "No matter if we're separated, and no matter how far away, I'll always be with you, watching over you."

Carla lay on the spongy floor sobbing uncontrollably, wishing Dad's words were true. And then another misgiving overtook her: was he still alive? She knew he was devastated over losing his wife and did not know what to do after injury forced him to leave Special Forces warfare; her father began displaying suicidal tendencies. Did he end his anguish? Carla prayed that he hadn't; if anyone could get her out of this living hell, it was Dad.

Nick was brought back into his pen by two Noids who tossed him onto his mat, where he bumped into the Plexiglas. Carla saw him clutching his groin and curling up in his rest area. She slid over the Pexiglass and wrapped her knuckles against it, getting Nick's attention.

"Are you okay?" she asked.

The handsome youth nodded. "The Noids tried too hard to squeeze more semen out of me."

Carla suppressed a snicker.

"What?" Seeing her smiling had Nick's high-wattage one coming alive.

Nick smiled weakly and mimed back, pressing a hand against the glass wall; Carla gestured the same handshake.

Finally, the handsome youth shut his eyes, falling asleep.

Carla thought this was no time to consider a guy cute.

CHAPTER 12

Dulce Base Laboratory

At Level Four, a room lit by blue fluorescent light didn't cast any shadows, as in a usual surgical suite that smelled of formaldehyde. Human doctors wearing surgical procedure masks and bio-hazard type protection suits operated on a Noid, its brain out of his skull and in a basin. It wasn't whitish gray like a human's, but dark. Another unconscious human was alongside the Noid on a gurney. They placed the Noid into an MRI-like machine—a pulsating red light began resonating in the skull.

In another section of the lab, two Noids on gurneys were wildly moving, one laughing hysterically, the other crying and moaning.

From a corner of the room in shadows, a female voice whispered in a hiss, "How is this procedure superior to the previous ones?"

One of the doctors answered in an evident mind-controlled monotone delivery, his face not having a stiff expression like the Noids'. "We must overcome the Pseudobulbar effect, characterized by sudden uncontrollable and inappropriate laughing or crying episodes. In other words, the way the human brain controls emotion.

"The machine makes the brain vibrate," the human doctor went on. "It'll assist in separating the bioplasmic body from the physical body...remove the soul life-force matrix of the human soul. Or in more simple terms, we'll 'kill' the human being but not its soul to use by us as a vessel."

––––––––––

In their desire to have human bodies as their own, the Rakers were near perfecting the ability to take a person's soul out of their body and put it 'elsewhere.' What happened to the souls? What is a soul? A soul was what made each human unique. The aliens referred to humans as vessels or containers. They contained a "soul matrix," or soul. Aliens work focused on extracting this soul matrix by machines using magnetic lodestones and then inserting the soul into another host body — another of their own.

Lamia inquired about the time frame needed to produce a disembodied soul successfully.

"Each operation moves us closer to harnessing the soul," the surgeon answered.

"How many more samples are needed?" the voice in the darkness asked insistently.

"Hard to tell. Perhaps another twenty, and we might succeed in better understanding the astral," the surgeon estimated.

"If it goes beyond twenty, you'll be patient number twenty-one for surgery to try and pluck out your soul. Do I make myself clear?"

"Yes."

"Good."

Lamia was well aware that her species lacked the feeling of compassion or love, unlike the human spirit. Lamia needed to understand better those that she would have absolute rule over. However, she intended to overcome that shortfall with systematic, step-wise incremental hybridization.

Lamia's brain was an ancient beast developed over one hundred million ago. The human neocortex came along a mere forty-thousand years ago. With the reptilian mind always on alert, the neophyte human brain proved no match. She knew Homo sapiens' vastly inferior I.Q.—a mere one-eighth of a Raker could never understand her drive to establish and defend territory.

From the dark shadows of the lab, Lamia noticed on a monitor surveillance El-Te walking along a corridor. She considered this ultra-rare Hubrid-3 a reject bogged down with human feelings, making him inferior to the H-1 and H-2 models. To Lamia, besides a human's precious blood supply, they were mentally inadequate, made bad enslaved people, and the list went on. Nevertheless, she realized Hubrid-3, like El-Te, was valuable in helping them understand the humans she would soon rule over. El-Te should be destroyed and started anew on the assembly line.

Dominance was central to the reptilian way of life. That supremacy over other life forms had proven a successful recipe for their survival and proliferation. However, as powerful as Lamia thought herself to be, she couldn't deny something very potent in the human spirit. El-Te would be an excellent place to learn more about its intricacies. To him, she conveyed mind to mind. *Meet me inside passage fourteen, room twelve.*

Yes, my Queen, El-Te returned telepathically from the corridor. He opened the door to the area directed. It was dark for Lamia to keep in the shadows.

Who is in charge here? She asked.

You are, my Queen, El-Te conveyed.

Lamia often played dominance games with the Raker males, challenging one another to see who was more robust. The contests would often get rough, with much biting and clawing. Yet as much as Lamia liked these jousts, she'd hardly ever played them with Noids and never with an inferior human.

Come closer, she traded thoughts. *I'm intrigued by the emotions humans have. Whereas our memories contain only information, theirs also include emotional memories. Why is that?*

El-Te answered. *It could be because Rakers were always biologically without emotions and have evolved that way. Or was it that deep in your past, they decided to rid themselves of their passions?*

Lamia thought about this. *Is it said we chose not to be troubled by the emotional imprints that humans have? Why are you troubled?*

El-Te deliberated before answering. *My emotional wiring is what humans call sensitivity.*

Lamia brought up: *I'm also a curious student of the social behavior of humans. Is that why your sex is often very intense because of the emotion called love?*

I, I don't know, El-Te conveyed.

Why not? Lamia asked.

I've never experienced sex with a human.

Lamia finally spoke in an audible whisper. "A rare Hubrid-3 like you have a singularly important attribute: you can reproduce with humans. You can have intercourse with them in a normal manner. You are barely distinguishable from normal human beings. Why don't you have sex with their females?"

El-Te followed her cue and spoke audibly. "I would if the act could be with a willing partner, not a brutal one forced upon a female."

"I'm a willing partner curious about human sex, and you are virtually human. If I want it from you, is that not willing sex?"

"I...I guess not," El-Te answered nervously.

"Do you want to continue living?"

El-Te knew well that the Controllers had him under

a trial period. He would remain operational if he functioned in some productive capacity. If he didn't perform, he could return to the tank; his parts recovered to start anew. However, El-Te was reaching the end of it all and became outspoken. "If my life is more of seeing humans dying the way they do here, I don't think so. My emotions cannot endure it."

"Then help me understand humans. Come to me. You've never seen me, have you?"

"No, I haven't," El-Te answered nervously.

"I don't wear clothes, for I also find them too tight and causing an unusual feeling," Lamia continued. "Many parts of my body are very touch sensitive. Imagine a normal human woman's body, and you have a good imagination of my body. Like you, I have a head, two arms, hands, legs, and feet; my body proportions are yours. As I'm female, I also have two breasts, but my skin is—" Lamia caught herself. "Come into the darkness to see for yourself, to stimulate your Queen."

El-Te's chest rose and fell as he stood motionless.

"Again, do you want to live?"

"Yes."

"Come to me." Lamia felt reluctant to engage in intercourse, sensing he wasn't attracted to her. To rectify the problem, she performed mimicry—shape-shifting in El-Te's mind and memory as whatever Lamia wanted, her induced image having nothing to do with her actual appearance. Telepathically, she turned up the sexual arousal mechanism in El-Te, manipulating his libido into an erotic dreamscape scenario.

In El-Te's sepia haze, images became planted into his mind; he could no longer fight off becoming aroused. Lamia contrived him to lie on his back, and she mounted him. Soon, ecstasy overpowered El-Te's emotions, and he, like female humans raped by male Rakers, could do nothing about it.

Momentarily, odd sounds emanated from the darkness—feral, wrestling, panting, pounding, wild moans, slurping, and sharp yelps.

———

Another Dulce base shift was over, and human employees went through the various security clearances before leaving the base.

"See ya tomorrow, El," Roger said to his best underground friend.

Once off the base, Roger called his wife like any guy on a job away from home. Roger became excited, anticipating spending the weekend with her and their little daughter. He had no idea that the Noids deprogrammed him not to remember the details of his work other than being a security guard/glorified janitor.

When the call ended, it was too early for Roger to return to his efficient apartment home. He went to the Wild Horse Casino and Hotel in Dulce to eat at the diner before spending time in their casino. Roger spent ten-dollars in quarters on the slots, video poker, and keno machine selections. Since working at the base, he was in the red gambling, but how could he ever forget the night he won fifteen hundred on the poker machine in the far corner? For some reason, he felt that tonight would be his lucky night.

———

El-Te's downtime from base duties was far different than Roger's. The Hubrid-3 craved a change of scenery, needing to erase his mind from the bizarre experience with Lamia. He wasn't sure if what had happened between them was reality or a dream. He couldn't rely on his mind for answers because Raker Controllers were strong in the mental environment and used to influence thoughts and feelings at will. They could project images, ideas, and emotions onto a person and accept them as accurate. If what he thought had happened to him, never in his wildest dreams could he believe his first time having sex would be with a Queen Bee Raker? He was so ashamed that he would never tell anyone about how she assaulted him, not even Roger.

His respite from his macabre existence became going to the library room to view nature films of the planet's surface. He enjoyed viewing movies of Earth's natural landscapes.

Sally had described some of her homeland of Oregon, enough for El-Te to imagine how beautiful the state was with its vast-ranging topography. He envisioned them escaping there to live—climbing mountains, hiking along the coastline, doing something on the water called kayaking, and viewing those beautiful valleys. The half-human also imagined them dining in a big city restaurant, all dressed up on a candle-lit table with a sumptuous meal in front of them, food that wasn't human-laced. El-Te's ultra-keen senses began wondering about his palette, savoring what she described. He also asked what a highly sought-after Oregonian Pinot Noir from the Willamette Valley tasted like, Sally's favorite fermented beverage. She talked of cranberries and earth flavors and a rustic quality.

Since meeting Sally, El-Te took such a genuine interest in terrestrial Earth that he soon realized that Rakers missed so much while concentrating on "eating and drinking" humans. Never did they, as Sally would say, "wake up and smell the coffee." However, that's what they were working on for their future.

Rakers didn't enjoy the earthly pleasures of drinking fine wine and other fermented beverages, sipping aromatic coffee, going to a sporting event, the opera, or whatever. They were just into the game of Extreme Predator, nothing more, like the one mammal on Earth famous for that—the Killer

White Shark. Just seize, eat, gulp; that was it.

El-Te's curiosity became piqued by humans having animals as pets, especially dogs. In the world he knew, that was unheard of; animals were merely a food source or to experiment on, nothing more. Of particular interest to him were German shepherd dogs. As he saw in nature films, their loyalty to their master was beautiful. He found it endearing that many people swear that a dog is the only thing on Earth that loves you more than he loves himself. They would even protect their owner with their life.

When El-Te finally left the library, he strolled near Holding Pen 33, as close as the current shift of guards permitted. Sally was lying on her cot, eyes open and staring at something only she could see. El-Te again felt an explosion of feelings overtaking him. Indeed, he knew that the most powerful of his brain circuits for pleasure became triggered by dopamine, creating delight inside him. It was true, he thought, that love was the greatest gift God created for man. Experiencing it for the first time, El-Te knew that from now on, his life would have no meaning or purpose without Sally. If he couldn't save her from the atrocities of Dulce, there was no reason for him to live, especially if he had to endure other sexual antics with Lamia.

Leaving the containment area, El-Te passed a large room filled with computerized gauges hooked to small tanks with tubing down into the tanks. The half-human noticed a humming sound, smelled formaldehyde, and the liquid was getting stirred in the tanks. Bile rose in his throat when a ghastly image came to his mind of Sally's remains tossed into the vat.

He hurriedly bypassed it only to come to another insidious scenario. Fertilized eggs of hundreds of healthy young human females were harvested repeatedly for unlimited embryos in their stem cell research, killing unaccounted human seeds.

Another lab along El-Te's route staggered the imagination even further. The rooms continued one after another, almost hollow, containing hundreds of tanks with gestating fetuses — their large, open black eyes dominating their tiny bodies. The tanks often became arranged in the gestational stages of development, from youngest to oldest. Fetuses removed from the abductees transfer to tanks filled with liquid nutrients.

Several newborns getting removed from the tanks seemed passive and even sickly. They didn't cry like human babies; there was no grasping with their hands, and their bodies were without the muscular tension of human babies. However, El-Te knew them to be far more alert than human newborns, wiser and more mature for their age. The totters could already communicate through their eyes as if absorbing information from the adults tending to them.

These atrocities were commonplace for El-Te to see, but they affected him now more than ever. Sally's days began to dwindle before she joined the list of hundreds of young women altered to become little more than reproductive cows. He'd have to save her from this, even risking losing his life. It's better to lose his soul than not do anything at all.

———

That evening, Hatchet's pickup truck stopped on the road. Brock got out and lifted the hood. Brock suddenly became wary when asking Sam inside the cabin. "Didn't they knock the snot outta ghosts in the movie Ghostbusters?"

"Yeah," Sam answered. "What's your point?"

"Just weighing my chances."

Feigning needing help, Brock flagged down one of the Rock vans while Sam leaned under the hood. It slowed, the driver's seat window wound down, and he started to rewind up to continue driving, but Brock got his meat hook hands on the Rock guy to pull him out through the window while Sam worked on overtaking the other man in the passenger seat. The two ex-soldiers unleashed a flurry of nifty mixed martial arts moves, knocking out the Rock men unconscious.

Sam nodded to his old war buddy. "What do I love more, your unique skill set or nasty attitude?"

"Just keepin' up Douglas MacArthur's credo," Brock said.

They repeated the mantra in unison: "Ours is the profession of arms, the will to win, the sure knowledge that in war there's no substitute for victory, that if you lose, the nation becomes destroyed, that the very obsession of your public service must be Duty, Honor, Country."

They lay the captives on the truck bed and slid a tarp over them. Sam then drove the men's surveillance van into a thick copse of pines.

———————

Inside Hatchet's cavern, extension cords provided electricity. One of the Rock men began to come around, and Doc took out a jar and cloth. "Ether. A little dab 'ill do ya!"

It knocked the hostage out cold. He went through the CAT scan, which detected a small microchip lodged in his head. Doc inserted an intricate rod into the man's nasal passage and worked to dislodge the chip.

The scanner slid over the other man, locating the same in his nose.

"Lucky for you, I'm an ear, nose, and throat man."

They blindfolded him on a gurney for Doc to insert a skinny fiber-optic tube into the patient's nose to examine the sinuses' openings visually. The fiber optic prober found the chip lodged very far in the nose, almost to the brain. It rattled when dropped onto a plate.

Doc gave a wry smile. "Let's see what these guys know when they come around without these little devils interfering."

They tied and blindfolded their hostages. Several filled vials on a table alongside them had syringes attached. When the first man came around, Brock set him in a chair and began squeezing him. "Remember my voice, the guy who just kicked your ass?"

"Ugh!" the victim moaned in pain. "Yeah!"

"It works like this...we ask questions. If your answers don't match after a shot of truth juice serum, I snap your fuckin' neck!" Brock looked to Hatchet, who turned on a small digital recorder. "Start recording."

Sam asked the man for his name.

"John Landson. Look, I'm a dead man if my superiors find out!"

Brock checked the man's wallet I.D. and nodded.

"They won't," Sam said. "Any pain inside your nose?" The hostage nodded. "We took out an implant."

"Didn't know I had one."

"He's probably telling the truth," Doc said. "They mind-swipe humans and reprogram them with Extremely Low-Frequency waves or drugs used to' encourage' them not to divulge the location or daily routine."

"It's true," the captive said. "Now that the chip is out of me, I understand I'm also a prisoner."

Brock asked, "These Controllers...who are they?"

"The ones at the base who give us orders."

"Are they the Rakers?"

"I don't know; I've never met them, never been in the base below the first level."

"I just saw a mutilated cow; its anus fuckin' gored out,

dick cut off, and testicle nuts lasered off," Brock said, his face a gruesome expression. "Gives me ideas on what to do to you if you're fuckin' lying!"

"I'm not! My job is to move people away from trying to get near the base. If they don't listen, we do away with them."

"Like me?" Sam asked.

"Yeah. Look, these creeps threaten my family, too!"

Sam took off the guy's blindfold to show him Carla's photo. "She was abducted six days ago near Archuleta mesa. Have you seen her?"

"I can't recollect. Only that another batch of new girls became brought in."

"Are they still alive?"

"Again, I don't know. I only —"

Brock grabbed him in a headlock, squeezing the man who screamed in pain. After several more questions, Doc stuck a needle into the hostage's arm, its syringe draining.

"Now I'll ask the same questions," Sam said. "Go over that again," he ordered. "Are you dependent on adrenochrome blood? Adreno?"

"All guards are," the Rock man answered calmly. "That's why we never miss going to work; we crave our next Adreno blood high when reporting."

Doc got into the questioning. "Don't you care that the blood you're feasting on comes from terrorizing young children and teens?"

"It's sick, I know," the captured man answered, "but they have us hooked on Adreno, craving its rush. A day without it, I get depressed. Also, our families will be in danger if we disobey orders."

Two Noids rocked Nick from his sleep, lifting him to his feet. He gave Carla a subtle hand gesture not to worry as they led him out of the pen. She hoped that would be the case. In this deep, dark, despicable world she was caught in, Sally and Nick were the only ones reminding Carla that she was still human. She couldn't deny her attraction to Nick's good looks and killer smile that stood out among this zombie world of the half-alive.

However, he tried to maintain a sense of humor even under these bleak conditions. Carla didn't even know what Nick's voice sounded like — nor did she care. She could sense it was a confident, powerful one. What he said was necessary, and she wanted to listen to his every word.

CHAPTER 13

Sam pulled into the Gilmore Apartments parking lot in the pickup truck with Brock. They saw the light in Roger's room and went to it, Brock knocking on his door. After a second, it opened.

"Yeah?" Roger asked.

"Hi. Town Welcoming Committee. Got a gift for you." Brock went into action, grabbing Roger in a wrestling hold. Sam stepped in with a rag doused in ether to put their newest captive to sleep.

At Hatchet's ranch, a Cabbit was sniffing around the cavern's entrance. Lone Wolf's sons circled it to entice it with food.

Los Alamos

The Shadow Group was in another emergency meeting in the mountain's secret meeting room.

"The Rakers are starting to bother me," General Blake grumbled. "Why do we have to do all their dirty work?"

"Because deals became made with them, remember?" Senator Warzon reminded. "Success, money, and power."

"Whoever has the gold makes the rules," Dennis Maloney said.

"We have security dead and missing now!" Blake said, none too pleased as he gave Major Briggs a piercing gaze. "We can't allow your Rambo to go on a rampage!"

Briggs tried to remain calm. "I warned you're messing

with the wrong guy. Sam Dawson will be a one-person army until he gets his daughter."

Blake glanced at several members before again addressing the Admiral. "Well, Dawson's in luck! They'll agree to give her back if he agrees to disappear."

Briggs considered this. "What's the catch?"

General Blake had it all figured out. "He'll be forced to sign an agreement never to go near Dulce again or go public about the base. If he reneges, the two Dawsons become targets until terminated."

"He doesn't trust us."

"But he trusts you. You'll be there to assure him."

Later that night at Brigg's Los Alamos home, he lifted his spiral red phone receiver and called. He heard Sam's taped message say: "Leave a message."

"Sam, it's Major Briggs. Your daughter's safe. I can get her to you..."

Military helicopters dotted the Dulce night sky, floodlights scanning the reservation terrain. Along the base's perimeter roadways, Rock men sentries at roadblocks inspecting vehicles.

————

Hatchet Cave

Sam was interrogating his captives inside the cave and remaining undetected as his old phone vibrated, but no one heard it. Roger, the third captive, began awakening.

Sam got close to him. "Roger? Roger? Wake up!"

Roger came out of it in a fog. "Who...? What's goin' on?"

"Remember me? I fixed your car?"

"Ah...Sam? What are you doin' to me?"

"We don't want to harm you," Sam began. Doc

displayed an implant.

"You knew you had this inside your head, right?"

"No."

Brock readied to apply pressure, but Sam waved him off. "We're gonna ask you some questions; nice the first time."

"Look, I took an oath under penalty of death that no matter—"

"You separated from your wife and little girl," Sam looked to Brock. "We have them."

Winking at Sam, Brock gave Roger a nasty smile. "Safe and sound...for now."

"What...? Why you—!"

"We won't harm them if you work with us." Sam showed Carla's photo. "My daughter disappeared six days ago near Dulce. Where is she?"

Roger studied the girl's face but didn't answer.

"Tell me, dammit!" Sam pressured. "Think of your daughter!"

"I...I don't know. Inside the base, hundreds of women, maybe thousands."

"Is Carla Dawson inside the base?" Hatchet asked.

"If she's there, Level Six be the logical place," Roger answered.

"How do we get to her?"

"Don't think it's possible."

"Would anyone inside work with us?" Sam asked.

Roger thought about it. "Maybe my Hubie partner... he's soft on one of—"

"Hubie?"

"A half-human Humanoid with some alien mix," Roger clarified. "His name's El-Te, who I call El, and he is heavy on human makeup, especially emotions. He feels bad for the prisoner girls." He added, "The Noids look at him as a defect, some retard, no doubt, with him struggling to contain all the human emotions inside him."

"You trust him?"

"Oh yeah," Roger said without hesitation. "El is different from the Noids because he's got compassion, and his intelligence is off the friggin' charts!"

"How smart?"

"Everyone's I.Q. is measured. I'm a hundred and seven," Roger said proudly. "El's is around four hundred! You speak any language; he'll have it down pat in five minutes."

"You talk of Noids, but what about the off-world species controlling things?" Sam asked. "You've seen them?"

"Nope, never. These Controllers stay in the shadows." Roger added, "El said the controller race of non-humans is called Rakers. Nasty other world mothers who call the shots below Level 7."

"From my research," Doc said, "these Rakers, as you call them, operate in fear. They need more understanding of the concepts of friendship and trust. Their society is one where everyone and everything gets monitored. To keep the upper hand, everyone in the base is somehow chipped, hypnotized, or mind-controlled."

"If you say so," the guard answered. "Kinda makes sense."

"Tell more about El," Sam ordered.

"He's part Raker but a very different hybrid. Rakers term El a rare H-3."

"Break that down," Sam requested.

"El had human parents," Roger answered, "but his pregnant mom, abducted by Rakers, added their DNA to the embryo. El still is top-heavy in a human's physical and emotional mixture. We both hate doin' the dirty work for the Raker fiends right out of some horror movie!"

Roger went on. "The only one down there that's got compassion. Jus' him touchin' a human, and he can tell much about what makes 'em tick. He's also clever to act like the other Noids, so they don't destroy him."

"What do Noids look like?" Sam asked.

"Very human-looking in the face and build, and their surgeons are working on perfecting them to pass for us. However, they need more work on uploading human feelings and emotions. Since the Noids don't have any, they are expressionless, like zombies; no one is home upstairs."

"Is that why all the experimentations on humans?"

"Yeah, El tells me their goal is to perfect these Noids to adapt to the Earth's topside and blend in with humans. Once they perfect these half machines, their assembly line will make millions of 'em take over the big Enchilada — Earth."

Roger next detailed seeing firsthand the gore of the Dulce vats corroborated former whistleblower Tom Costello's story: the off-world species' subsistence required human blood and certain biological substances of theirs to survive. In extreme circumstances, they could exist on bovine fluids. Food is converted to energy by chlorophyll through photosynthesis, and waste products become excreted through the skin. The aliens also found certain human hormones that helped them withstand Earth's environment better.

"Tough as hell for 'em to live on the surface 'cause of the biological and bacterial contamination risks," Roger said. "So they stay most all the time Below Level Seven."

Sam's group looked at one another with deep concern.

"What else?" Sam asked.

"Rakers get high off human adreno blood, and the Noids crave it, too."

According to what Roger knew, animal abductions had slowed a bit since some government labs began the production of artificial blood for Dulce.

That didn't appease Sam. "If that's the case, why did these pricks take my daughter then?"

When the captive had no answer, Sam asked with bitterness, "Are the creeps below inseminating girls?"

"Some of them, yeah. The off-world ones take the male sperm and put it into the captive girls. When the pregnancy hits three months, they insert the embryo into an alien female."

"For what purpose?" Doc asked.

Roger rubbed his temples. "I don't know what to believe anymore. All of it sounds like some far-out science fiction stuff."

The guard also admitted feeling that human medical people were working in the Dulce Base labs. He believed these men, primarily surgeons, probably didn't know they were programmed or mind-swiped not to remember a thing when their shift was over. It was like they were conditioned not to have any compassion for the humans they were carving up.

The interrogation continued on other matters, with Roger admitting, "You're gonna think I'm smokin' peyote, but El-Te sez these Raker dudes have mastered atomic power. Like they can go through walls as we go through water."

"I get that way too from certain mushrooms!" Brock said with a snicker.

"Believe it or don't believe me."

"What about their underground weaponry?" Sam asked.

"I don't know about Rakers, never see them, but the Noids use a gizmo called a plasma flash gun. It looks like a flashlight and is easy to operate. On the side of it are three recessed knobs in three curved groves."

He explained the Noid "Flash" weapon operated in three different phases. Like Star Trek, Phase One could stun and kill if the person had a weak heart. It can levitate anything in phase two, no matter what it weighs. Phase three was the *strict business* mode, used to paralyze anything that lives, animal, human, alien, and plant, or on a higher frequency that could kill humans instantly. The most vital position of phase three of the Flash would vaporize anything that lives, leaving no trace of what it made disappear.

"So bulletproof vests are useless?" Brock surmised.

"Yep. Wearing protection or not, a phase three zap will turn you into crispy bacon on a skillet."

Roger alerted of a form of sonic used for security. Built-in with each light fixture was a device that could render a man unconscious in seconds with nothing more than a hushed tone. There were still and VCR cameras, eye print, hand print stations, weight monitors, lasers, ELF and E.M. equipment, heat sensors, and motion detectors at Dulce. He also made known that magnetics controlled everything at the underground facility and that electricity was obsolete. That included a magnetically induced illumination system.

Roger continued his rant. "El-Te says the Controllers ain't military powers, so they don't do a show-for-force thing. The tricky bastards know a far more effective takeover is possible through secretive infiltration, manipulation, and persuasion, which they can accomplish without firing a single shot."

"He's right," Doc agreed. "They're devious, employ deception, have no intention of any apparent peacemaking process, and don't adhere to any prior arranged agreement. This method is a matter of their culture, which trickles down to personal values. Lies and deception are valued ways of negotiation, and agreements don't mean crap to them."

Doc gave some eerie statistics concerning alien supremacy. "Why is one in forty Americans estimated to be implanted? Some believe perhaps even one in ten. These zombies—have been programmed to help overthrow Mankind soon. That's why aliens want to share advanced technology with some humans in key positions of power. They're accomplishing that, and their agenda has begun to manipulate the population as a whole."

Talking freely now, Roger switched subjects to confess of El-Te wizening him up about the many humans they encountered in cages, usually dazed or drugged and often emitting inhuman shrieks and wailing noises. El told Roger that the Noids became led to believe these young prisoners were hopelessly insane and disturbed and prone to outbursts, involved in high-risk drug tests with them. Roger and the human guard had orders never to try to speak to them. Initially, he'd believed the other Noids about this story, but El-Te knew otherwise. They were wholly sane; on the outside, their people searched for them without success.

Sam's group looked at one another with a sense of dread.

"What do they do with the cow blood and other parts from mutilated animals?" Sam asked.

"Do they need these fluids for research or survival?"

"All the cattle mutes goin' on around here is due to those underground needing cattle and human blood," Roger admitted. "They extract genetic material for breeding purposes to fine-tune their race and Noids for Earth living. El sez cattle chromosomes are nearly identical to human chromosomes."

"You said breeding purposes," Sam asked. "Are they impregnating the captives?"

"Yeah, some of the girls, those sicko bastards," Roger said with bitterness. "It's true; the Raker's big goal is to hybridize our species and take it over."

Sam finally asked, "How can we get to their Raker

Controllers?"

"Don't know that you can. Not only do Rakers stay hidden below Level Seven, but they can melt through matter. As I said, I never saw 'em but now and then hear their voices givin' my instructions."

"Is it one Controller or many?" Sam asked.

"Several of them," Roger admitted, "but the Queen Bee, according to El, is a female named Lamia."

"Lamia," Sam spoke the name out loud as if testing its sound. "Give me details."

"Some girls can break a guy's heart, but Lamia supposedly can tear it out and make sandwiches!"

Doc changed the subject. "The chip in your head is how they communicate to you."

Sam became perplexed. "If Rakers are so smart, how does El-Te go undetected by them?"

The Dulce guard said that when he and El-Te arrived at the feeding area. Roger goes with human workers to eat regular food, while El-Te eats with the drone Noids. "Here's an example of El's cleverness. Humans eat in one feeding area, and Noids at another."

The Noids went to a feeding vat—a large container with a mechanical arm stirring the red-colored broth.

"Noids drink the slop using ladles," Roger described. "Noids consume a human an' cow gland solution. El fakes swallowin' it and on the sly spits it out."

Sam kept the interrogation going, getting Roger to tell of the daily occurrence of Noid and Human security terrorizing cages full of children and young adults, chasing down victims screaming in fright. They catch prey and use needles and syringes to collect blood from the base of their spinal column and necks.

What the security guard admitted next made Sam

cringe even more.

"So many young girls on Level Six that it's called "The Farm," Roger went on. "A new shipment of 'em brought in is known as the "Lolita Express."

"Harvested for high-octane blood?" Doc asked, and Roger nodded.

"Where do they abduct all these young victims?" Doc went on. "From shopping malls, refugees an' immigrants tryin' to cross into a country, kids from war-torn an' natural disaster areas, most all disappear unnoticed, soon forgettable."

"But not our kids!" Sam said, clutching onto Doc's arm.

"Amen," Roger answered in sympathy. "Rumor has it that Rakers has been child poaching for decades, ever since realizing they aren't the only ones lovin' adrenochrome. Some high-rollin' humans look the other way of this butcherin', all jus' waitin' for their next fix."

Sam asked, "So Rakers use it to control high-powered people?"

Roger nodded. "If El can believe, which I do, yeah."

Brock took out his knife to stab it into the table.

"Well, Rog," Brock spit out, "you better learn to function without it, play ball with us, or else you're gonna meet your Maker soon!"

A panicking Roger looked at Sam. "Christ, muzzle this Pit Bull! How can I fuckin' help you when needing rabies shots to be near him!"

Brock didn't let up. "These Raker scum must have weaknesses. Talk!"

"Good luck with getting to 'em. Thousands of security camera monitors an' tripwires so sensitive a fart can set 'em off!"

Roger told of once walking through the Nightmare Hall corridor, hearing screams from those held captive, banging on the Plexiglas, and yelling:

     " —We're not insane!" " —These monsters a—" "Please help us!" "They're lying to you!"

CHAPTER 14

Dulce Base, Nightmare Hall

Inside Cell 33, two Noids stalked a cute Asian teen girl, ignoring her frantic screaming, and dragged her into a lab room. Through the Noids' eyes, the Controllers observed the hysterical girl.

"What… what are you going to do to me?" the girl asked, panic filling her voice.

Noids situated the teen on a cart, strapped her arms down, and their device read her "fear count," which went wild.

These Noids transferred thoughts to a Controller; *She's a highly live one.*

Good. Juicy, sweet blood, a whispery male voice communicated back.

"Keep away from me!" the girl screamed. Her calls, this time, turned into screams as the Noids tore off her robe. Two others strapped the teen onto a gurney and then moved out of the way. Just as the lights dimmed, a door opened, and several figures in shadows approached.

Right before they blindfolded the girl, all she saw coming out of the shadows was a three-toed bi-pedal creature advancing until she felt a bony hand rubbing against her skin.

"Get your dirty claws off me!" she shouted.

How can we? She heard in her mind. *Your fear is so irresistible.*

The other Noids in the room agreed in mumblings.

"Get away, you freak!"

Freaks? the lead Controller in shadows, unseen, asked the girl's mind in surprise. *What's the difference between a human and a cow? You are nothing but livestock.*

Another Controller in darkness had his mind communicating; *cows have no fear!*

I shall breed with this one, the lead Controller decided, pleased. As the gurney wheels lowered, he climbed atop her as screams died in the girl's throat.

A Noid finished with his pleasure and dismounted from her. She was wheeled to another area that looked like an opium den where tubes ran out of several girls' veins to release blood that plumed into a mist over shadowy creatures absorbing it into their skins as if at a health spa! Minutes later, the girl was unconscious on a gurney, her legs splayed open.

––––––––

Hours later, the Asian girl returned to Cell 33, tossed onto the floor, the door slamming shut behind her. Several prisoners, including Carla and Sally, helped the bludgeoned victim to help her onto a cot and gave her water.

"Part of me wanted to die on the spot," the girl said to them with a moan. "To sink beneath the ground and stay there. But another part still hopes to be saved, able to hug my parents again."

She rolled over, curling herself into a ball, shielding herself from the world. The unimaginable rape trauma she endured was evident.

A chill ran through Carla, thinking she had already narrowly dodged a bullet like this several times. However, the odds were against her; it was inevitable that her time was coming.

––––––––

Hatchet Cave

Captive Roger continued interrogation, answering their questions. "Noids aren't good decision-makers unless in a group," he confessed.

"Okay, got that," Sam said. "What else?"

"They're photosensitive; any bright light hurts their eyes. That could be a weapon against them, but they recover quickly."

"I brought flood lights," Brock added. "We'll blind the fucks."

Sam continued. "What else can help us?"

"Come check this out."

"No funny stuff," Brock warned.

Roger got up to scuff his foot and picked up a small handful of dirt. "Point a flashlight in the air."

Sam complied, and Roger flung the fine particles into the air, where they floated about in the light.

"Dust messes 'em up their Raker side big time," Roger informed. "Makes breathing difficult for them, sometimes get sick an' die."

"Can we get dust blowers?" Brock asked.

"If not, leaf blowers will do the trick," Roger added.

"How can we penetrate the base?" Sam asked.

"No one has! The only openings are for their crafts to come and go."

"That's our breach!"

"Think again," Roger corrected. "Hydraulics close 'em as instantly as a whore's spread legs when she doesn't get paid."

Talking freely now, guard Roger told of 1,700 paved underground roads at Dulce and Northern New Mexico and another 800 miles of tunnels and corridors towards Los

Alamos. The base was still growing due west. Roger claimed he saw nuclear-powered tunnel machines that burrowed through the rock, deep underground, by heating whatever stone it encountered into molten rock—liquid lava—which cooled after the device moved on. The result was a tunnel with a smooth, glazed lining. These underground tubes used by electro-magnetically powered sub-shuttle vehicles could travel at incredible speeds, connecting to other sub-city complexes.

On Roger's crude map, he pointed out manufactured images on Google Earth maps, although the resolution needed to be more precise. Nevertheless, everyone could make out the base's massive redundant power supply systems. Everything above ground seemed dedicated to power generation and distribution of air handling for something else underground to whatever was below and deep. The behemoth fans were to exhaust toxic gases and maintain breathable air below.

Sam's team eventually took a break from the questioning and had Roger draw a crude map of the central part of the Dulce Base. He explained the schematics of the base that the First Level started at 200 feet from the surface. Each level had a ceiling of seven feet, except levels six and seven; the roof was 45 and 60 feet. There were approximately 45 feet or more between each base level. The average highway ceiling was twenty-five feet. The Hub at the base was 3,000 feet.

Comparing Roger's map to the one a year ago by guard Tom Costello proved they were amazingly similar. The underground multi-level base itself was as large as the city of Manhattan. The first three levels contain government offices and a garage for street maintenance. The second-level offices also had a garage for trains, shuttles, tunnel-boring machines, and UFO maintenance. The third level is mainly government offices.

Doc put his finger on the map. "The fourth level is to conduct research and experiments on the human psyche, dream manipulation, hypnosis, and telepathy. All aspects of mind control programming take place here as well."

"Yeah, some weird shit goin' on there as well," Roger said.

"Like what?" Sam wanted to know.

"They can lower a human heartbeat with deep vibration waves of some kind—Delta, I think," Roger answered. "It makes a static shock, and then they reprogram the brain somehow to put data and all kinds of stuff into your mind."

Doc weighed in on this. "The development of Bio-technologies like this would mean a revolutionary change in the life of every human being on Earth."

"Yeah, but fewer humans needed to make the change," Roger quipped. "Remember, El said they wanna wipe clean Earth of ninety percent humans."

"Unless we can throw a monkey wrench into their plans," Sam said.

Doc glanced at his notes. "The scientist Bennewitz, who was first to report an alien species living under the Archuleta Mesa, had what he called the most practical way to break into Dulce. The first move would be to close the dam's gates above the Navajo River, the water route held closed for the duration. Internal to the one cave, there's a small dam for water storage. Its capacity is small."

He pointed to a map coordinate. "This discharge outlet downstream could be closed, causing wastewater to return to the caves. The water is vacuum pumped from the river by electrostatic means."

"So he said to cut off their water supply to wear them down?" Sam asked.

"Yes, the Controllers need water to survive, to run their machines," Doc continued. "There's a water intake and dam upstream easily cut off, and the water re-routed to Chama, New Mexico."

He located it on the map. They discussed more logistics to pull this off but began to see the negatives.

"If there weren't hostages inside, the plan could work," Sam said. "But cutting off the water puts the prisoners at risk and my daughter."

The plan became nixed; they looked for another possibility.

Sam pointed to Level 5 for Roger to enlighten them. "Most of that level is Noid sleeping quarters," Sam started. "But on a wing of Level 5, witnesses have described huge vats containing amber liquid with human body parts constantly stirred by a robotic arm."

"That's a fact," Roger began. "In rows, thousands of cages held men, women, and children to be used as food and put into these vats for the underground bloodsuckers."

"Fucking sick bastards," Brock mumbled in disgust.

"We already know the sixth level is "Nightmare Hall," Doc continued. "It contains the genetic labs, where the crossbreeding experiments of humans and animals get conducted. Right?"

"Yep. For sure."

"What else?" Doc asked. "Give it to me between the eyes."

"Nightmare Hall," Roger said with a sense of doom. "From the tunnel entrances there, starin' down at you are carved gargoyles and winged beings, spooky as shit, and livin' up to its name."

Roger detailed the genetic labs and crossbreeding experiments of humans and animals that were conducted there. "Betcha, it's the largest crime scene in the world. They look at humans as ignorant lowlifes but discovered a Metagene — a gland in the human head not used much, Pinoli gland, I think."

"Pineal," Doc corrected with a smirk. "What's the significance of metagene?"

"El-Te sez it's able to awaken in people under emotional overstress or real strenuous physical activity to create superhuman abilities." Roger thought more about it. "The Controllers are tryin' to tap into this metagene. If not, people all jacked up on this can be human shields or warriors to help fight their battles if anyone attacks them."

"Describe Level Seven," Sam demanded.

"Cryogenic storage...row upon row of the dead preserved mostly in solutions."

Roger pressed his temples to recall more. "Some get stored in clear cylindrical containers over six feet in height. On the same level, humans are everywhere in cages behind bars, waiting their turn to enter the house of horrors — Nightmare Hall."

Sam's emotions took another time when hearing this on a roller coaster. He pushed back the negative to ask, "El-Te said Below Level Seven is the Raker hive. Below Level Seven leads to a vast Hidden Empire of sun-city complexes."

"Betcha DUMB bases are called that just to mock us!" Brock spat defiantly. "They think they can do all this secretly and that we were too 'dumb' ever to figure it out. Those fucks are wrong!"

Hatchet Chalma's sons entered with the captured Cabbit in a cage and showed it to Roger. "Betcha, you've seen one of these before."

"That's just a little critter from the big zoo down d'ere. How did you — ?"

"Every so often, one escapes," Hatchet explained. "I followed one through this cave. Deeper in, I saw it about the base after we crawled through a small hole. A big metal door and something alongside it lookin' like an air shaft."

"That's right. Everything works down there on magnets, which they call lodestars. But all doors are powered by big ass magnets. Rakers get off the vast magnetic power surging through Earth."

Roger told this off-world species coveted the strength in the power of magnets. They believe magnetic energy is more valuable than any other thing on the globe.

Sam punched his fist into his other palm. "My heart defibrillator…electrical or strong magnetic fields can mess it up, cause interference. Have to steer clear of them."

Doc understood the reason. "Magnets can activate a switch which can prevent the ICD from delivering treatment therapies to the heart such as life-saving shocks. Somebody must reprogram your device, and I can't perform that procedure."

Sam pushed away from his heart problems to get back on track, asking Roger, "You mentioned magnets controlling their doors. Can they be bypassed?"

"If you were to place a large electromagnet on the entrance, it would affect an immediate interruption. They'd have to come and reset the system."

Brock just won the lotto. "Bingo! That's our breach! Hit that weak point, make surgical kills, use surprise and confusion, and put the creatures into a cluster fuck!"

Roger became wary. "Not so fast. Every shaft has cameras and bars that seal off the hall when the magnets foul up. You still couldn't go anywhere. And the door only unlocked for a minute 'til the nearest guard resets it."

"That'll be *you!*" Sam said. "You opened these bars

before to reset the door, right?"

"Now, hold on! The deeper I go in the base, the stronger the security. When their machines detect no chip in me..."

Doc had a ready answer. "I'll re-attach it, and you return like nothing's happened."

"But they'll know what I'm doing. Shit, they can read a person's intent! Under the death penalty, I swore I'd never divulge the info, no matter what I saw or heard. Man, if they find me guilty of treason, they'll turn me into a puree an' dump me into a vat!"

Doc began calculating. "Your friend down there that you trust, El...is he chipped?"

"I don't know for sure, but I doubt it. El's one of 'em, more or less."

Doc moved closer. "Convince El to remove yours once you pass security."

"Way too risky. His human part might want to go along, but what if his alien side says no? You won't be there to help me."

Doc studied the group before him. "El is our only hope."

"Play on his human compassion," Sam advised. "Tell El-Te what'll happen to your daughter if he doesn't help."

"If he rats on me..."

"Think of your little girl!" Sam added, "El has to realize this could be his only chance to free the woman he cares for."

"That could work," Roger figured. "He's fallen for a human gal inside. I say he's in love with that pretty one."

"*Ah-ha!*" Brock nearly screamed. "Tell him she'll die a gruesome death if we can't rescue her."

"You're not the bad guy, Rog," Doc insisted. "Not your fault for what they're doing."

Roger was a beaten, nervous man. "I'm fearin' you

guys are gonna hurt my family."

"We won't, Rog, promise," Sam said. "Soon, you'll be back with them. Why do they live in the Las Vegas area and you in Dulce? Is she your ex like mine?"

Captive Roger said that many human workers were from out of state, brought in daily from one-hour flights out of McCarran Airport Las Vegas on unmarked 737 jets; the workers returned to their shift's conclusion. Roger was the exception to this. Deathly fearful of flying, he was allowed to use an apartment in Dulce. He'd drive back to Nevada on his two days off to see his family, so programmed to say he had a regular, primary security job at a military base.

Roger, on a break having a beer and smoking a cigarette, saw how desperate and grieving Sam was, willing to employ any means necessary to get his daughter back safely. "I feel for you," hostage Roger lamented. "Hope you hit on some info' I've given that'll help hunt down these ruthless suckers."

Sam appreciated Roger's words. "I can't stop hearing the clock ticking down on Carla. It's the worst spot I've ever been in, and I've been in some tough ones. But they were a piece of cake because only I die. But my daughter killed..., no."

Roger put a comforting hand on his shoulder and spoke for everyone to hear. "Controllers control everyone independently but often take hours to make a group decision."

Brock thought about that. "I say we surprise them, attack the fucks before they can work things out."

Roger broke out, shaking.

"You okay, Rog?" Sam asked.

"Well, not really," he answered. "Hate to admit it, but my body misses its Adreno fix. I hope this cold turkey you guys have me under will help me break off."

Los Alamos Mountain Area Tank Room

The Shadow Group was heavily into another emergency meeting in the underground Los Alamos Tank Room.

"Two guards dead, two missing!" General Blake blurted unpleasantly to Major Briggs. "We can't allow your Rambo to go on a rampage!"

Briggs worked to remain calm. "I warned that he's the wrong guy to mess with. He'll be an army of one until he gets his daughter." Again, he told the men that Dawson had enough muscle, brains, tactics, and daring to face and defeat countless enemies.

"The Rakers have it all figured out, or so they say," General Blake informed.

Upon the meeting's conclusion and the apostles' moving about to other areas of the tank facilities to continue in preparation for the Culling, General Blake called in a tech assistant to speak to alone.

"You said the glitch in Briggs' microchip is no cause for alarm?"

The young techno-nerdish guy knew his craft. "No, sir. Every apostle gets a recheck of their chips. None dislodged. The Major's chip interruption was the first time."

He brought up that some microchips failed due to microscopic cracks in the weld connecting the antenna, leading to the microchips or leakage of the glass capsules, resulting in fluid accumulation around the microchip. Also, a microchip implant subjected to a solid electromagnetic current may cease functioning.

When he dismissed the technician, Blake heard the familiar female voice. *A Judas in our bunch can ruin everything. Isn't it better to be safe than sorry?*

———————

Sam noticed a blinking light on his old cell phone. Listening to Briggs' message had his eyes lighting up.

Sam and Brock wore protective vests and carried weaponry as they left the cave in the ice cream truck. Twenty minutes later, out on the Res in a lonely spot, they seemed in the middle of nowhere.

Sam got out of the truck and used his phone. "Hello, Admiral."

"Sam!" It was Briggs on the other line. "They assured me your daughter is unharmed, but I don't buy them saying she wandered into a secure area."

"That's pure bullshit, sir!"

"Do you care as long as you get her back?"

"What's the catch?"

"You sign an agreement never to go near Dulce again or speak publicly about the base. If you revoke it, you and your daughter will be hunted down and terminated."

Sam smelled something. "Seems like a perfect setup to take me out."

"Then take precautions; wear belt and suspenders," Briggs advised. "I'm on a chopper to broker the deal at your location. Contact me when you pick the place to meet."

CHAPTER 15

In the study of his home, the military man, Major Jason Briggs, set the Red phone back on its cradle. The magnets and adhesive tape once again attached across his nose bridge. Going over the gravity of what he was about to do, the faint sounds in his head disappeared. He felt relief knowing he controlled his mind for the twenty minutes he had.

Briggs took out the legal pad, flipped over several pages of his handwriting, and continued with his whistleblower disclosure.

The Major, so immersed in getting every revelation he could into the letter, had utterly forgotten about the time constraints he was under; he was about ready to be at the twenty-minute safety limit of the microchip detected unattached.

Briggs stopped momentarily to run a sleeve across his eyes, becoming moist. *He thought, "I wish I dared to stop this madness* before jotting it down. "…However, the Controllers have leverage over all of us. If they realize what this letter discloses, I will reach the end game, as would my wife. If this letter goes public, I implore former Special Forces soldier Sam Dawson and Senator Paul McNair to ensure my wife gets protection. I can only hope that in the darkest moments of humankind's existence, you two will find the heroes inside of you who must rise, as I am, to save the planet from the ashes of the world we once knew."

Jason Briggs attached a printed list of Shadow Group names and high-priority DUMB base locations.

Finally, the Major realized the time with the magnets attached to his nose had exceeded the twenty-minute maximum by nearly a minute. He quickly took off the strip of tape across his nose.

"Jen?" he called out. "Come here."

His wife, a young-looking sixty-year-old with a tight natural body and becoming face, came into his study. However, her usual cheery face turned severe when her husband's eyes swelled with tears.

"What's going on?" she asked, studying his face.

"I'm fine." The Major took her hand. "I'm being picked up in twenty minutes. Come outside."

Briggs brought her to the patio deck and lifted a loose tile to expose a small square hole. He took from it a cellophane package and showed three manila-sized envelopes posted with various mailing addresses. One was to Sam Dawson.

He handed over a sheet of paper for her to read, pressing his index finger against his lips for silence. Jen read the page:

Should anything happen to me tonight, immediately certify mail these. One is for you that will explain everything.

Jen began losing it, whispering, "What...what's going to happen to you, Jason?"

The Major kissed his wife's hands and her lips. "Oh, nothing, just ol' phobia me being super cautious. Do you understand my directions?"

"I do."

He set the patio tile back in place and held onto her. "In a couple of months, our Hawaiian paradise will be ours; no more military, right?"

"Yes," his wife said, unable to stop tears from rolling down her cheeks.

"Good," the Major said, wiping them away. "Our new

life will begin."

———

"General, sir," an assistant called Blake at home.

"Tell me."

"It's Major Briggs. The second time his chip has malfunctioned in three days."

Blake listened to how, just yesterday, the microchip in Briggs' head became short-circuited for a few minutes. No big deal; it happened to almost all of them at one time or another. But two malfunctions of Brigg's chip just a day apart, never.

"Very strange," the assistant deduced. "The only means this could happen is if the Major or someone else disconnected the chip."

"Are you sure?" Blake asked.

"Yes," the assistant confirmed. "The chips are failsafe otherwise."

"That will be all," the General responded, sending the assistant away.

Blake knew well the consequences when a soldier performed high treason during an imminent threat of war. Major Briggs, one of his most trusted soldiers, was a traitor. Never would he have expected that until Sam Dawson showed up in Dulce. As Briggs had done, Dawson rose through the ranks based on merit. Briggs also was the one who promoted Dawson for bravery in combat, which spurred morale and invited a cult-like following for these two cuts from the same cloth.

Blake smelled a rat, a giant rat. To Blake, it was evident that Major Briggs wanted no harm to come to Dawson. The General could understand that, but Briggs had crossed the line.

———

Sam stared into the night before returning to the truck and

driving off. In fifteen minutes, they were at a previous cave where Sam had searched for Carla. The sign-out front read: Prairie Dog Cave.

"The passageways leading out of here are like Swiss cheese," Sam said.

"Do your thing," Brock answered. "I got your back."

Shortly, they made preparations for the meeting. When they drove into the cave, they put on Night Vision goggles. Brock had an automatic scope and a shoulder-launched portable missile launcher. Sam positioned himself at the cave's entrance on a nearby mesa cliff.

Sam saw two headlights approaching vans while an Apache helicopter carrying rockets descended on the cave entrance. Major Briggs hopped down.

"Stop right there!" Sam shouted.

"Easy soldier," Briggs cautioned. "Let's do this peacefully."

"Where's my daughter?"

"In one of the vans."

From the chopper, the Pilot and other black-attired passengers watched Rock guards spring from the vans. A shadowy presence hovered at the edge of the Pilot's vision as if watching the scene with "eyes and ears."

The Rock surveillance men fanned out to surround Sam.

Briggs became shocked by what was unfolding. "What's going on here?" he asked. "Where's Dawson's daughter?"

A Rock security man fired a revolver into Briggs's temple, instantly killing him. An angered Sam shot an arrow into the killer's chest, dropping him. Brock fired his automatic from the nearby mesa, killing several of them as others sought cover while the helicopter fired back a missile at Sam. He rushed inside the cave just before it blasted the entrance. A second blast from a rocket launch from the chopper shattered boulders into a small avalanche, burying Sam inside.

The copter followed Brock, who grabbed his FIM-92 Stinger surface-to-air shoulder-fired launcher, setting its sights on the helicopter. The missile blasted the chopper into a fireball, twirling and crashing to the ground as Brock rushed off.

Sam was running, but a pain in his heart slowed him, which dropped again to catch his breath. No verification of Carla being alive had him sinking lower than low, but adding to its weight was his dear friend, Briggs, trying to be peacekeeper, KIA. Sam sprinted through the labyrinthine cavern, feeling he would go mad over this all. Another blast at the entrance shook the whole cave, and he thought everything might crash down upon him. He continued, trying to locate an exit, but his light had begun to expire. Soon, he would be enveloped by the total and almost palpable blackness of the earth's bowels, just as his daughter might be.

Don't fucking do this to me, God! he thought. *Don't let me die like this, not without Carla out!* The air in this cavern was hard to find, stifling.

It was then that Sam's flashlight grew dim. He shook the light to see if the batteries had become jostled, but it didn't help. Instead, the light went out as if a wire had dislodged. He heard a growl and footsteps as he stopped to try and fix it in total blackness. An animal had obtained his scent. The tension in his brain became frightful. He took a Special Ops tactical knife from his belt, ready to play the night moves game. He could hear the animal's labored breathing, seemingly as terror-struck as he was. Next, he heard a yelp and another— different from the previous one. He realized it was a mother mountain lion or something akin to one, protecting her cub. *I have a child, too,* he said to the animal in his thoughts. *You defend your babes. I don't want any trouble, won't harm you.*

Sam felt a slight breeze across the right side of his face, away from the animals. It must be a cave opening. The air felt good to breathe. Ever so carefully, he crawled to the crevice leading to the surface.

———

Nick wrapped on the Plexiglas divider. Carla was sleeping, but Sally heard it and awakened.

"You've got the nerve ribbing me about El-Te," Sally said, nudging Carla. "What's with you and the Super Sperm guy?"

Carla sprang awake. "Can't I at least fantasize about a beautiful life beyond this place before I end up being someone's supper?"

Sally patted her shoulder. "Sure, kid. Go for it. He's handsome and seems nice."

Carla slid over the dividing glass, gushing at Nick. "So…if you were to take me out," she asked, "where would we go?"

"Not cave exploring!" he quipped.

"Amen to that!"

"Med school tapped my savings," he mouthed. "But not before I bought a piece of land on Catalina Island."

"Where's that?"

"Just about thirty miles from the southern California coast." Nick gestured grandly with his arms. "Two gorgeous acres overlooking the Pacific Ocean."

"It sounds great!"

"Someday, I want to build a house there," Nick said. Meantime, I'd take you there and cook us a meal on the grill."

Carla's eyes moistened upon pressing her hand against the Plexiglas to touch his. "My bags are packed."

Nick, caught up in the excitement, continued, "We'll

camp out under the stars..."

Carla became in awe as he described how beautiful things would be for them. She found herself putting two fingers to her lips, kissing them, and then placing them on the Plexiglas, Nick doing the same.

Sam and Brock returned to their cave base camp to detail the ambush and Major Briggs' demise to their team, deeply saddening Hatchet Grey Wolf. "I can't believe they killed him; so expendable to them."

"He simply knew too much," Sam figured. "But who gave the order to off him?"

"Doesn't matter; he's dead," Brock lamented.

"I'm back to square one with my daughter," Sam lamented, his shoulders slumping.

"Don't do this to yourself." Brock bumped shoulders with him. "Don't forget our motto: *De Oppresso Liber* — To Free the Oppressed."

Sam shook off negative thoughts of Carla, the other soldiers once under the Major's command doing the same to proceed with their plan. Following the Cabbit animal and Roger in tow, they navigated Hatchet's maze of corridors cave with four cavern rooms. Nature filled them with speleothems of decorative rock formations forming stalagmites and stalactites. While passing flowing limestone and cave pools, the trail, rugged and in many places, was highly slippery, forcing them to climb up smooth and slick flowstone using a hand line. Crawling through a small opening in the next chamber led to the massive metal door, which disappeared through the bars of an air intake panel. Behind it, an air shaft rose into the rock.

Roger studied it. "It opens on Level Five, Hubie housing. Place the magnet —"

Just then, Sam raised his hand for silence when he heard a distant sound deep in the shaft. "Hear that? Listen."

They leaned their ears toward the shaft and heard moans and screams.

"That's comin' from below, Level Six," Roger said in a pained voice. "Nightmare Hall."

Having digested so much about that slaughterhouse area in such little time, Sam had horrific images invading his thoughts. All things twisted, heinously twisted.

The admission turned Sam into an emotional wreck, choking up alongside Roger.

Sam admitted, "The fuckin' truth is I came to the Res to bag a Bighorn before offing myself."

"Why do that, Sam?" Roger wanted to know.

"My life's dead. The military and my wife are both done with me. All I have, Carla. If my little one doesn't make it, I don't wanna live!"

Hatchet put a hand on his shoulder when he became emotionally overcome. "If she's inside, we'll get her out." He finally pulled his sergeant away.

"Best you do the raid when the Noids change their three pm shift," Roger advised. "They'll be in a little disarray."

Upon returning to their Lone Wolf Cavern outpost, Sam, Brock, and Doc stood over Roger, splayed out on a table. "Do your thing, Rog' and never forget our daughters."

Doc gave him ether before re-inserting the implant into his nasal passage. After completion, Sam and Brock, again in Indian disguise, drove to the Gilmore Apartments in Lone Wolf's car and helped groggy Roger into his room.

Los Alamos Mountain Retreat Tank Room

The battle of wits between Sam's team and the Above the Law

government group continued. The Shadow Group was again in a heavy debate at their hideaway retreat.

"They found several openings at Prairie Dog Cave that Dawson could've escaped from," the nerdy scientist delivered.

General Blake was none too pleased. "He's still out there...with backup!"

A CEO asked, "The media wants to know why the military blasted an Indian Reservation cave. Especially when Native American tribes are sovereign and have exclusive inherent jurisdiction over their territory."

The general considered what ruse to use. "Issue this report. Intel confirmed a terrorist plot to bomb Dulce. We cornered the bastards in the cave and took care of business. The military sealed off the area until confirmation of no other threats!"

Sam's team continued studying the Dulce Base map on a table. "Timing is everything," he said. "We get in, get out."

Doc text messaged his wife. *Judy, I am Commencing assault tomorrow. Contact media and bring it to Hatchet's ranch cave at the coordinates given. Love you, Doc*

The group began rechecking their weapons and gear.

On the Main Street of Dulce, folks were observing heavy military artillery passing through town, including tanks, Jeeps, and heavily armed soldiers. Closed-circuit T.V. cameras were also monitoring the perimeter of Dulce. Throughout the Jicarilla Apache Reservation, search party flashlight beams abounded as military vehicles moved about. Above the reservation, helicopters flooded the area with bright lights and noise.

Inside the chopper, SWAT soldiers monitored things using sophisticated sensor equipment. Thermal imaging scanned the terrain below, picking up heat signatures.

———

Karen Dawson was again on the phone with Doc's wife. "Judy, how have you endured wondering if your son is alive?"

"I haven't. Some days, it's too painful to get out of bed."

"If I can't try to help save Carla, I've no reason to live." Karen began breaking down. "My marriage...I lost Sam, but still love him."

Karen, finding a comforting soul in Judy, confessed that when a soldier comes home, he often brings back the war with him – emotionally, at least. Karen knew well of the clinical studies confirming what many people had long suspected: the families of soldiers who had lengthy and repeated deployments to Iraq and Afghanistan suffered much more.

"It all was a continuing stress," Karen lamented over the phone. "Carla and I were at a constant ready force. Sam was either leaving for another tour or returning from one, only to leave again, a real emotional roller coaster for everyone."

Sam's absence, combined with his wild mood swings when home, led to Karen seeking a lending ear when he was gone. However, that only led to a bigger problem: an affair with another man and then another.

Judy felt the woman's sorrow and made a decision. "We're both mothers with the same problem, so listen. Can you get to Lone Wolf's ranch undetected? Somebody might be following you, so you can't take your car."

"Friends of mine have a Piper Cub plane," Karen said excitedly. "They'll help me."

"Good," Judy said.

CHAPTER 16

The heartbeat of Roger's chest turned into a pounding jackhammer as he re-entered Dulce Base. He passed through the usual security inspection gauntlet, including microchips and retina readers, before moving past the human workers doing their daily chores as Noid guards monitored their activities.

Roger located El-Te, whispering, "I'm in trouble, need your help. It's my—"

"Daughter," El-Te finished for him. "I sense your need."

"I'll never see her again, an' you won't see Sally unless—"

"Stop. Your plan has a flaw!"

Several miles from Hatchet's cave, he, old Billy, and Sam faced a band of Indians in a tribal meeting while scouts became hidden on the lookout.

Hatchet whispered to Sam. "It's like riding into Bethlehem with you, the Chosen One."

"Skip the anointed talk. Just a father after his daughter."

Old Billy stepped up to speak to his tribe. "Nevezgane returns to war against the Sky People!"

"Damn…there he goes again," Sam muttered.

"Show 'em some proof, Nevazgane," the old Indian said.

Murmurings among the Indians had Sam begrudgingly taking out his bow to concentrate on something in the distance.

Drawn on a high mound of clay nearby was the shape of a person. Sam's arrow hit the figure in the heart. Indians let out War Chants.

The ex-Special Forces soldier motioned to speak. "For years, Sky People have taken your loved ones, and now my daughter!"

"This is war!" Hatchet added. "We finally take a stand and claim back our land!"

More war chanting came when Billy helped pass out bows and arrows with flint heads and knives. Their mantra stopped when they heard a warning howl from an Indian scout on a hill. Sam quickly concealed himself before a rocket-armed helicopter hovered over the tribe, and a dark van pulled up with two Rock Men getting out. They approached Billy Two Snakes, holding snakes in each hand, doing a tribal dance around a fire.

"What's going on?" A Rock man asked.

Billy stopped, caught his breath, and gestured to the figures drawn on the nearby rocks. "Prayin' to our Gods. Don't you have one to pray to?"

The Rock security men were emotionless, looking over the bows and arrows before driving off and the helicopter veering away.

"Dumb-ass, numb-nuts palefaces," Billy muttered.

───────

Just outside the Dulce town limits, Brock was inside the True Value Hardware Store asking a clerk, "You got some real strong magnets?"

"How strong?"

"Somethin' to hold fuckin' King Kong!"

As sunset began washing over the desert, the sun disappeared below the line and, in parting, gave a medley of colors turning yellow, pink, and rose. Finally, it sank, and the atmosphere dropped; the bright color began to darken into lilac and purple and then disappeared entirely.

The helicopter activity increased their floodlights everywhere. Several strange lights in the night sky streaked about Archuleta Mesa, zooming at incredible speeds until disappearing.

Level 6 – Cell 33

A half-asleep Sally held little Gina like she was her mother. Lying near her, unable to stay awake any longer, Carla slumbered.

Nick moved closer to the Plexiglas divider, not wanting to awaken her, for he knew the constant strain she was under when the Noids came back on the hunt for high Adreno count girls.

The handsome youth studied Carla's high cheekbones, full lips, and sparkling eyes.

Under different conditions, he knew he wanted to be with her for a long time.

Noids on the Nightmare Hall floor heard in their minds: *Cell thirty-three compromised – deception detected among females. Catch them off-guard.*

Sally went into her zombie routine too late. The door opened without the clicking/unlocking sound. The Noids rushed in to catch the girls off guard, the screaming mayhem beginning again, Sally this time dragged away. Sally's screams awakened Carla, who became grabbed by a Noid, ripping at her robe. The shrieking continued to echo throughout the holding pen.

Nick pounded on the Plexiglas in frustration when witnessing her dragged away. He slid to the floor, unable to hold back emotion.

_____

Last-minute preparations began in Hatchet's cave: Brock testing magnets, Hatchet preparing bows, arrows, and tomahawks, all tipped with flint.

"Flint weapons will poison 'em," Billy said with assurance.

"Doc," Brock, chuckling, pointed to Hatchet. "Tell this loco Injun that flint arrows don't have magical powers, just another Indian superstition."

"Don't be so sure," the medical man answered. "Flint produces dust, and some rare earth metals are toxic. Lighting matches give off toxins. Poison for aliens? Who knows?"

Hatchet rubbed the dust onto arrow tips, spears, tomahawks, and knives. "Once flint enters alien bloodstreams, legends tell of the nasty things happening to their blood."

Sam's team noticed helicopters filling the evening sky from the cave's entrance.

"They'll track our body heat when everyone gets here," Sam said.

Suddenly, they heard animals bugling and snorting in the growing darkness, hooves scraping the ground. They put on Night Vision goggles to view a herd of Big Horn Elk.

"What the...?" Brock didn't understand their presence.

Hatchet explained, "According to Billy, the Earth Mother wants to help us Indians...and Nevazgane."

"Here we go again."

Billy came outside the cave, sniffing the night air. "Elk wait for many moons for revenge against the mountain creatures from the deep."

Brock rolled his eyes. "Chief doesn't quit."

"Maybe they can run decoy for us, distract the choppers."

"C'mon, Sarge."

"They'll know what to do to help," Billy assured.

Brock was amazed. "Who slipped me LSD?"

A helicopter passing by carrying a Lieutenant and a SWAT team observed the buildup of heat signatures on the screen. Suddenly, a bald eagle appeared in the choppers' lights as it buzzed the cockpit.

"What the hell..." the miffed Pilot shouted.

The Lieutenant snickered. "Hey, give that bird some space. That's our national symbol! There's nothing here but elk. Move out."

The Pilot veered the chopper in another direction.

The sky was completely black in another hour, but the choppers were back, their lights sweeping the sky. Sam and Brock, fully dressed and equipped, wearing Night goggles, hid near the cave entrance. Suddenly, the elk herd, even more prominent now, took off in one direction with the choppers following. With the sky currently empty of floodlights, Sam's team opened the entrance for two dozen Indians coming out of hiding with bows and knives.

Brock was confused by the joined resistance group getting bigger and bolder. "Did someone slip me fucking 'shrooms or what?"

Inside the cave, the group with the newly arrived Indians carried gear as they advanced toward the Dulce Base air shaft.

Brock couldn't fathom their resistance group getting bigger and bolder. Some used tomahawks as their primary weapon. "Holy hell! We're about to fight an enemy with high-tech weapons and go in with Stone Age stuff."

He gave Billy an apologetic look. "Chief, sorry for not believin' you. I do now. We could've used you on some of our Special Forces missions."

"War missions? I know all about 'em," Billy said.

"How so?"

"Korean War, a code breaker with the Apache and Himmarshee tribes."

Brock saluted to the old Indian with new-found respect. "An honor to meet you, soldier."

———

Roger walked alone along several long, gloomy Dulce base corridors, fearful of being watched. Did he imagine it, or were Noids peering at him around corners? With extreme anxiety, his constant companion, he made it to a section of the tunnel just out of range of a camera to duck inside a dressing room locker, looking at his watch. Seconds later, El-Te also slipped in.

"You scared me!" Roger whispered nervously.

"Contain your fear and negative thoughts," El-Te advised. "Quick, lie down. I'll remove the device, but leave the component that allows them to communicate with you." He took out an odd-looking surgical device.

Roger became emotional. "Thanks. My daughter, I live for her."

El-Te couldn't contain his own emotion. "The Controllers detected Sally's deception. Precious little time. Hurry!"

———

Sam's team reached the Dulce underground air shaft door, where they calibrated their watches. Super magnets were attached to the large metal doorway. A klaxon alarm sounding had their tensions ratcheting.

Sam again checked his watch. "One minute and counting."

Hatchet signaled everyone to attach water-soaked handkerchiefs around noses and mouths to keep out the dust and other particles once they began to rain upon the enemy.

The klaxon alarm timed to go off just as Roger and El-Te were to be near the air shaft opening.

Roger spoke into his transmitter. "Door ninety-six malfunctioning. Permission to reset the magnets."

Brock continued pumping himself up, punching his chest. "Let's get it on! Time to let the dawgs out!"

"Proceed."

Roger and El-Te swiftly departed in a tunnel to traverse the expansive corridor.

"I'll never forget this," Roger said. "If I don't make it..."

"Stay brave."

"I ain't no hero."

"Your compassion is a mighty weapon. My spirit is with you."

Two Noids were already there when they arrived at the shaft's malfunctioning door, starting to raise the bars blocking the way. The entry for Sam was just beyond.

"Oh, shit. Now what?" Roger asked.

"Stay brave. I will be near you." El-Te then spoke to the Noids through mind transference. *It's all right. We will reset it.*

The cross-mix breed was about to leave when they heard a noise outside the door through the air intake shaft.

What was that? A Noid asked telepathically.

I thought I heard something, too. El-Te communicated telepathically. *Let's raise this.*

As Noid security ascended the bars, Hubrid-3 El-Te, acting with great speed, snapped both of their necks, and they dropped to the ground. Roger, shocked to the core, quickly followed El-Te.

The Lieutenant and SWAT team aboard the helicopter hovering over Lone Wolf's cave saw a peculiarity: various news trucks and media began gathering.

The Lieutenant got on communication. "Sir, we got a situation here!"

People featured in the chopper's low beams on the media were Doc's wife and Sam's—Karen Dawson.

In the Dulce Base air shaft doorway, Brock pumped up and guzzled the contents of a beer bottle, smashing the empty bottle against his head and shattering the glass. "*Hoo-rah!*"

The magnets did the trick in the Dulce air shaft doorway, and Brock pushed it open, punching his chest. "I'm in beast mode; let's fuckin' get some Noid scalps!"

Sam's team, followed by a crowd of Apaches and Indians from other clans, burst through the door past the surprised Roger, who held the bars open for them. In a moment of decision, the captive guard joined them.

Floodlights, dust, and leaf blowers had the Noids repelling, gagging, coughing, and shielding their skin. Automatic rifle fire, Indian flint weapons ripped into them— the flint poisoning taking immediate effect.

Hatchet threw a tomahawk and then another, slicing into the foreheads of Noids. Other Indian arrows with poison also worked to have the Noids staggering about before dropping to the floor. Eagle talons and razor beaks ripped into enemies' heads as Elk sharp horns gouging also do heavy damage.

Sam rapidly fired with his bow, flint-tipped arrows hitting targets. Brock smacked around a Noid with wild-eyed, maniacal glee, tossing the creature into a vat of blood in maniacal delight.

"A dozen Noids put to bed! These fuckin' weirdos are like hemorrhoids to me!"

CHAPTER 17

The Tank, Los Alamos Mountain Hideaway

The covert Shadow Group heard over communication.
"They've breached Dulce! Repeat—"

"Shit!" General Blake cussed. "How could this happen?"

The Noids attacked inside the Dulce base and began firing off their laser plasma guns with a blue beam. One levitated an Indian warrior as he turned into a gristle and dropped to the floor. Several Noids began fleeing the melee, hopping onto a bullet train and whisking them away in a flash of super speed.

"Take out the rail!" Sam shouted just before the over-amplified magnetic power in the installation began to make him dizzy and light-headed. He clutched onto his heart, forcing it to push onward.

Brock tossed two grenades, their explosions collapsing debris onto the tracks. The invading team continued to penetrate, making it to Level Six Nightmare Hall while killing more cross-mixes. As they'd hoped, confused Noids resorted to retreating mode; some died before the others fled into their rabbit holes.

Sam began searching the cages full of women for Carla. Doc also surveyed the prisoners, screaming and begging for help, looking for his son.

Sam's squadron continued down the first corridor.

A group of Noids fired Flash guns. A beam levitated

an Indian warrior, frying him before dropping him to the floor. Sam's squadron continued systematically down the tunnels—the Indians communicating in a unique dialect amongst themselves, the Special Forces soldiers using their com-code.

Another colossal door opened suddenly to release more Noids. Still, the Indians continued the rapid-fire arrow shooting, slowing them down until cross-mixes began doubling over and dropping to the ground as the flint, poison to their systems, took effect.

Several Noids fled the melee, hopping aboard the lone maglev train, somewhat battered but still functioning, and whisking away.

Sam waved his troops to another Holding Pen area containing more young women and some young men. "Evacuate them out!" he yelled. "Also, use the air shaft!"

Brock broke open the locks to begin helping the screaming and weakened humans out of confinement.

As the ex-soldiers and Indians battled their enemy ferociously, Sam began searching the holding pens for Carla, Doc, for his son amid the pleading screams from legions of prisoners.

The invading troop ran through a tunnel illuminated by phosphorous to reach another holding pen area filled with young adults.

The sheer magnetic force in the base began to weaken Sam's heart device. He felt dull chest pain and some in his left arm before feeling like an elephant was sitting on his chest. He worked to fight off symptoms to push on, witnessing hundreds of females screaming for help. "Evacuate them!"

A weakened Sam continued, obsessed with locating his daughter among the sea of battered women. "Carla! Carla!"

Flint-tipped Indian arrows hit with thudding sounds

into Hubrids, the poison also working to have them staggering about before dropping to the floor. Tomahawks also landed on the backs and heads of the enemy.

Brock broke open a Holding Pen lock. A Noid fired off a blue beam, hitting an Indian, opening him up like a fish, and burning his shoes right off him to leave his remains smoking.

Roger appeared as bows and guns were ready to take out El-Te. "Don't shoot! He's El-Te! DO NOT SHOOT!"

Sam ordered his squad to Stand Down, and they lowered their weapons.

El-Te asked Roger. "Where's the girl's father?"

Roger pointed out Sam. El-Te placed a hand on the soldier's chest. Inside the human/alien brain, synapse components moved at an unbelievable speed through a complex maze, deciphering Sam's DNA. El-Te also mapped his heart, the emotions it houses, the pacemaker defibrillator, and its leads going into heart veins. Gleaning the necessary information, he motioned, "The solid magnetic forces in the base will damage your heart further. Leave now or —"

"Not without my daughter!" Sam shot back resolutely.

"This way." El-Te dashed off.

Now leading the group, the half-human half-alien rushed into a scene of ghastly genetic crossbreeding experiments. In one section, an unconscious young man's head opened up mid-operation. At the same time, female abductees, cold and naked, were splayed out on other tables, long probers snaking up to their legs into groin areas, awaiting the inevitable butchery.

Sam dashed off, and the assault team followed him to a bio-genetic lab.

The attacking team began setting captives free, and some who had trouble walking got assistance. A small deployment continued onto Level Seven, passing a mechanical arm stirring vats of red with cattle and human parts inside, like a stew with meat!

His squadron began breaking the locks to release the prisoners while El-Te guided Sam and others to a vast reinforced door. "Your daughter's inside." He also detected someone else's vibrations. "And my Sally is with her!"

Sam, further sapped of energy, pushed on the door to no avail. When Brock lent muscle, it finally gave way. Just as Sam, helpless, stumbled inside, the door speedily slammed closed, magnetic locks snapping shut. Several Noids wrestled Sam onto a gurney, binding his hands and feet.

"Daddy!" Carla shouted. She was tied to a gurney and was next in line to have her blood drained. Behind her and doomed to the same fate were Sally and little Gina.

———

Brock began pounding on the door from the outside with El-Te and the Indians.

So, now I have the ringleader! The female Controller voiced on the inside from the darkness, speaking directly into Sam's mind in a whispery voice.

"I just want my daughter," Sam pleaded, "and we'll leave."

The violence in your mind excites me, the Raker female conveyed. *Bring this troublemaker to me. Forget your friends outside. None of you are a match for our vastly superior intelligence.*

"Just let her go; you've got me," Sam pleaded audibly.

But she will give us pleasure, perhaps offspring, the Controller conveyed without words.

A needle into a vein opened in Carla's arm, blood dripping into a large vial. Sam watched helplessly as several of these cross-mixed Creatures began drinking it and passed a vial to the Controller. "I thought you were intelligent," he said in disgust. "You're just junkies, junkies addicted to human adrenochrome!"

Just as humans are addicted to our technology, the Raker Controller answered wordlessly. *I believe you call that co-dependency!*

Sam displayed fear for the first time when the Noids put a monitoring device on him and transferred him. *He is their leader.*

He will pay.

"Fine," Sam said. "Open me up and drink all you want; just let my daughter go!"

A Noid began drawing Father Sam's blood.

Your rising adrenalin count excites me, the Raker transmitted with glee.

"You're pathetic!" Sam shouted. "Certainly not a mother to anything!"

He faked being scared and panicking as a syringe drew vials of blood from his arm. "No, don't! Stop! I can't take this!"

"I love you, Daddy," Carla said in a choking voice.

The Controller conveyed to both their minds – *the human soul...so caring, so willing to sacrifice one life for another.*

"You heartless bastards don't understand!" Sam seethed.

Our emotional life is limited. So we experiment with yours, working to acquire it.

"Daddy!"

Sam heard in his mind: *Perhaps I will take your big, brave heart. Transplant it inside me. What would that feel like? As tasty as her luscious fear?*

"How can you rip people apart, ruin their lives?" he asked. "So heartless."

The Raker female continued with the conversation audibly. Her clawed hand emerges from the darkness, a finger pointing his way. "Please. You are a soldier; all you know is to kill. I see your hands and weapons have slaughtered hundreds of humans, and you say we are cold-blood killers without compassion?"

"War is over for me," Sam admitted. "Let her go free; do what you want with me!"

"You, finished with war? Never!" conveyed Lamia. "You're a machine addicted to killing. Able to murder someone, sleep, and forget that it ever happened. It became customary for you to be that way."

"I was doing my job, that's all!" Sam shot back.

"Humans are nothing more than wild animals, killing each other and the planet," Lamia gave back. "War isn't horrible to you; a life-and-death fight is the only thing that makes you feel truly alive. You had to cultivate explosive anger to survive in combat. The adrenaline rush is tremendous, just as our rush to drink your blood is. You killed some of my soldiers and made you feel great. Don't lie, for I will know if you are."

"If you didn't steal my daughter, none of this would be happening!" Sam seethed.

"But it did. I've had enough of your low-life nuisances needing to be under control. We will diminish humans greatly; the ones allowed to live will be a slave race," hissed Lamia. "Humans, nothing more than farm animals. The way you turned out is what happens when an experiment goes wrong."

When Sam's blood filled a liter container, the Noids passed it around to drink, handing some into the shadows for Lamia. However, the Noids all began to cough violently and gag immediately.

Smacking his lips in disgust, one of them conveyed to the Controller. *Flint!* He then clutched onto his stomach, dropping to a knee before collapsing onto the floor.

"Flint! Deadly to your kind," Sam shouted to all.

Brock became maniacal outside, trying to break down the door. El-Te waved him off to study the door in deep concentration. Inside his mind, synapses spin wildly as numbers and formulas whizzed through his brain in an attempt to decode the door. El-Te's mental efforts finally produced a click from the door. Brock and company rushed inside to dispatch several Noids before they could fire quickly. Sickened by Sam's blood, these robot-like creatures slowly fled and were shot down by guns and arrows as Sam became untied.

At the room's far end, the female Raker stepped out from the shadows to grab Carla as a shield. It was the queen bee reptilian herself — Lamia. Nearly seven-feet tall, Lamia is "para-human" — partially mixed with scant reptilian features — greenish skin and large yellow eyes with vertical slits. Thin-clothed, she was well-proportioned with an alluring figure and moved like any two-legged human, pupils vertical slits. A sleek utility belt wrapped around her waist.

Lamia's long, pointed finger gave off a laser beam of light. Now, she spoke audibly to her enemies. "If this touches her, she dies."

Sam signaled his troops to back off as Brock tossed him a gun.

The blasting flood lights exposed the female Raker — Lamia. The Raker Queen rapidly developed skin burns from the intense UV floodlight rays.

Lamia dragged Carla to a massive, uniquely fortified door. Choking and gasping, she spoke aloud. "Don't try to follow me. Below Level Seven will end all human life on this planet!"

Her three-fingered claw hand extended a long finger, emitting a laser beam close to Carla's neck. "We are no match. Is that what you want to hear?" Sam asked, seemingly defeated. "I will leave a defeated man; just spare my daughter!"

Lamia, weakened by flint poison and floodlights, struggled to hold a deadly finger to Carla.

Sam, untied, aimed his gun in a showdown.

Lamia spoke to El-Te. "Why didn't we kill you at birth? So filled with human DNA!"

"And you, Lamia, feel nothing for anyone but yourself without a soul," El-Te returned. "So pathetic."

"You have no soul," El-Te answered aloud. "I am not like you!"

He didn't waver. "There's nothing to you other than a larger brain. Humans have so much more to offer. We've no use for your type who aren't trusted, have no soul, an uncaring heart. You're nothing more than a psychopath, an emotional predator. What you want from humans goes far beyond drinking their blood, possessing their bodies, or having sex. You must feel powerful, possess, and destroy humans, bodies, and souls. A real-life vampire is all you are!"

"You're just another drone slave!" Lamia said, her anger coming through. "Humans are as valuable as weeds."

"Not so," El-Te countered. "You fear us because you know we're potentially powerful beings, yet you insist you own us. All you've done is create a lie."

Sensing Lamia growing weaker, Brock moved closer, thirsting for a kill to flash the light close to her face; welts began forming.

"You don't know anything!" Lamia hissed.

"I know humans' greatest strength is their belief in God," El-Te went on, "our connection with that one Supreme being. Rakers pose as a god; you're *not* Him, but Lucifer's Fallen Angels—God's rejects!"

Gagging and hissing, Lamia warned, "This battle isn't

over!"

She swiped a hand across her utility belt in a super move, changing her molecular structure to disappear through the door.

Carla stumbled to the floor as El-Te rushed to untie her, Sally, and child Gina.

Sam managed to pick up his daughter, holding onto Carla dearly. "Those constipation pills you gave me; the flint inside them just saved our lives."

El-Te went to Sally. "You made me want to be a good human, to get to know you outside this hell."

"I would like that," she said, holding onto him.

Everyone fled the room.

The fight continued on the Level Six corridor, but the Noids were the only ones supplying opposition, Rakers unseen. However, the cross-mixes Noids dropped fast as the flint-tipped arrows continued to pierce their flesh. Brock noticed a Noid gun at his feet. He shot a beam from it that levitated a boulder and dropped it on the Noid with a splat. Quickly deducing how it worked, he saw a wounded Noid trying to escape and take care of business.

Until a strange occurrence occurred: a bunch of Noids suddenly yanked on wires from their chests to ignite detonation blasts that blew themselves into flecks of red.

"Shit!" Brock yelled. "They erased themselves."

"Man, what a mess!" Hatchet added.

"Their way of getting rid of the evidence," El-Te said. "But I'm alive, proof that these aliens live here."

Brock saw another Noid ready to pull on a chest cord but stopped when given a command that only he heard. He pointed his Flash Gun at El-Te, but Brock pushed El-Te out of firing range and began stalking the Noid, who also successfully blew himself up.

Sam's team, including Roger, Carla, Sally, and El-Te, opened more cages to allow inmates to escape. Hundreds of dazed and confused human abductees staggered out of the cave into the air shaft door, into Lone Wolf's cavern, and to freedom. Doc and Billy lingered at the entrance.

"We're out of here," Sam ordered. "Move it, or get buried under this mountain!"

"We're going back in," Doc said, standing with Billy. "I have to know about my son."

Billy said: "My woman's probably dead, but—"

"Hurry before they regroup!" Roger cautioned.

Sam studied the legions of abductees and told Hatchet, "Get your warriors to help them outside!"

Hatchet jumped to it as Sally spotted Carla. "We made it!" The two women hugged one another dearly.

"Didn't I say my dad would do something?"

CHAPTER 18

Sam's squadron joined in as they hurried back inside Nightmare Hall, passing the mangled carnage on Levels 5 and 6 and continuing to LEVEL 7. Once there, they proceeded to the Cryogenic Storage, where a seemingly endless row of unmoving people floated in tanks filled with a liquid the color of peaches.

Sam stared in wonderment. "Who are they...Who *were* they?"

"The unlucky ones at Dulce," El-Te solemnly replied.

Another holding pen contained multi-armed and legged humans, some drugged, others groggily moving about. Doc studied a young man and began banging on the Plexiglas. "Nick! Nick!"

The handsome youth turned to see his medical man's father and his blank face shone with a glow as Brock smashed and opened the door, as father and son hugged.

"How did you find me?" Nick asked. "I'd given up on ever getting out!"

Doc looked at Carla. "Her Special Forces father saved you!" With trepidation, he asked, "Are you okay? Did they —"

"I'm fine." Nick hugged Carla. "We're fine."

To Doc and Sam's surprise, Nick and Carla embrace with a heartfelt kiss.

Billy studied the many human specimens in the amber solution until they stopped at a particular tank. His face took on shock and awe when he gaped at the same naked, beautiful dead woman that El-Te had previously shown Roger.

"My wife, White Cloud," the old Indian said teary-eyed to Sam.

"I'm sorry, Billy. She was beautiful."

"Ain't she? My pride. Finally, we're united."

El-Te entered to stand alongside old Billy, everyone noticing the resemblance of their facial features. They studied one another before returning their attention to the naked woman suspended in the tank.

"She was my mother," El-Te made known. "You are my father!"

Billy nodded in wonderment, his eyes welling with tears. "This is so great."

"I was removed from her womb and harvested."

El-Te and Billy were initially hesitant to embrace each other before going into a full hug.

Sam noticed a monstrous vaulted blast door at the end of the room, giving off a strange life force.

"You wish to know what's beyond Level Seven," El-Te said. "Deep caverns extend for hundreds of miles. It's their headquarters for taking over the Earth!"

As Sam, El-Te, Doc, and the rest ran to exit the base, entourage in tow, El-Te detected a pale-yellow viscous liquid pouring out. "Nitroglycerine explosives meant to destroy this base and all its evidence! Get outside now, or else we become buried here!"

El-Te added, "We must take a Noid, dead or alive, as evidence of what is happening here."

"But you're alive," Sam told the Hubrid-3, "proof that these aliens lived here."

Two Indians began dragging out a deceased Noid.

———

The helicopter hovering just above Hatchet's cave had SWAT soldiers repelling to the ground. The Lieutenant viewed the multitude of evacuating prisoners coming outside the cave as they felt blessed relief for the first time in ages, all filmed by a T.V. crew.

General Blake on communication with the chopper's Lieutenant. "Do you have a visual of Dawson?"

"Yes, sir."

"Take him out! Now!" Blake ordered.

"But, sir, T.V. crews film everything. Killing Dawson, a decorated soldier, do you want that going worldwide?"

Sam, being congratulated by the hordes of escapees, looked defiantly into the sky at the chopper as if baiting them to fire.

"God dammit!" General Blake shouted.

Doc's wife was also haughty on the ground, throwing the soldiers aboard the helicopter the middle finger!

Karen rushed to Sam, hugging him lovingly.

"Thank God you're alive!" she said, teary-eyed. "I couldn't stay home with you two in danger."

"Mom, I'm moving in with Dad," Carla finally announced.

Karen weighed the decision. "I won't stop you. I'd do the same if someday your father could ever find it in him to forgive me."

Sam forced down the lump in his throat but didn't respond.

With Sally and child Gina, El-Te trailed the herd of fleeing abductees.

"Don't get captured by humans!" Sally pleaded. "They don't understand your kind yet; you could be imprisoned or executed as a part of this evil!"

"She's right," Sam agreed. "For the time being, go into hiding until this blows over. No one has seen you, so we will say you are one of the unfortunate killed inside the mountain.

I'll find you and help to get you safe."

"What of our life together?" El-Te asked Sally.

"Listen to Sam until it's safe for you!" she said. "I love you and don't want to lose you. Go into cover! Hurry!"

El-Te kissed her intensely and hugged little Gina as if the child were his own.

And then he took his first hard look at this strange new land called surface Earth.

———

Deep in the abyss of the Los Alamos area mountain hideaway, General Blake and his Shadow Group felt the tensions becoming palpable when viewing a large screen of the event at Dulce. A helicopter hovered over Archuleta Peak, considering Sam leading a massive human evacuation out of the mountain. T.V. screens showed the same image on all channels.

A Shadow Group CEO businessman noticed the Red phone on the desk had an insistent blinking light. "The White House."

"Fuck the President!" Blake yelled. "No one knows anything of us!"

The nerdy scientist ran a hand through his hair. "I hope so. No one will understand the pressure. They'll say we're the bad guys — traitors!"

———

Minutes later, Archuleta Mesa emitted a loud, deafening rumble that, as the mass nitroglycerin soaking the six levels of the underground base, had it buckling. The mountain coughed up plumes of debris and then settled atop a smashed-to-bits Dulce Military Installation Base.

———

At a Dulce Health Center, Doc worked from a makeshift operating facility alongside other surgeons and workers using long devices to extract implants from the base prisoners. More abductees lined up in the hallway, waiting their turn while communicating with relatives and friends.

Doc took a break in another room for coffee, sitting alongside a local doctor offering assistance, "Once the implants get removed," he said, "let's hope we'll be able to deprogram and rehabilitate most of them back into society."

"Will they remember the horrors gone through?" the assistant asked.

"Hopefully, not even in their nightmares," the assistant added.

———

That afternoon, as Sam continued reuniting with Carla, he received a call on his original phone from Major Briggs' wife, Jen.

Sam began to say, "Oh, Jen, I'm so sorry for your loss..."

"We need you now!" Jen said, panic lacing her voice. "My husband left something for you. No time to delay! Oh, God!"

Sam heard some brief details before ending the communication when he alerted Brock and Hatchet, who walked over. "I sense the bad news."

The three former Special Forces soldiers took on a look of puzzlement.

Sam went to his ex and Carla. "We have to put out another fire."

"Don't, Daddy," Carla said, holding onto him. "We're safe. Isn't that enough?"

"You two safe? What a great feeling for me," Sam replied, hugging them both. "But America has a thorn in its side that we guys will pull out."

An Apache helicopter arrived minutes later to lift off Sam's small assault team.

Security guards were about the perimeter of Major Briggs' home and gave Sam and his team access to enter. Widower Jen Briggs became forced to control her emotions as she got down to the gravity of her husband's confession.

"My husband feared his group might silence him," Jen began. "The lengthy letter he left behind named names to the group, how they sold out to the aliens and of their nightmare plan."

She disclosed how her husband predicted that if the Dulce Base became breached, it would self-destruct to hide the evidence. "The pressure Jason was under," she lamented, "he just couldn't take any more of being silent about the atrocities."

Jen's cell phone rang. "It's Senator McNair." Jen broke down, handing the call to Sam. "Let him tell you. It's a safe line."

"Sam Dawson," he said over speakerphone.

"We don't know each other from Adam, Sam," Senator McNair began, "but Major Briggs trusted you and me — Senator Paul McNair."

"Tell him, senator," the widower of Jason Briggs advised. "Everything."

McNair's voice took on an ominous tone. "The Major detailed in his letter the group of government people, industrialists, and others working with the Controllers at Dulce."

The Senator insisted. "While we send troops to the various DUMB bases about the country, I need to strategically position you guys in striking distance to cut off the head of the beast."

He gave details, with more to follow later, before the communication ended. Jen displayed her husband's meticulously drawn map. "There's a secret exit route from the Tank Room's installation under White Rock only reached by super rail. However, outside is a hidden emergency exit constructed only after a recent storm flood."

The helicopter took Sam's four-person assault team to the White Rock Canyon Rim Trail 6,300-foot mesa summit. Briggs' map led them to a sizeable faux boulder that looked natural. Behind them, a cluster of bushes concealed two doors: a hatch-like doorway measuring three feet by three and a personnel door seven feet wide, eight feet deep.

Sam's team concealed themselves behind boulders. Monitoring the time, he said, "If it fails, we move in."

Several levels below White Rock mesa near Los Alamos, a glum General Blake sat in the tank Room with his Shadow Group apostles. They heard more dire news of several of their huge strategic underground facilities becoming barricaded.

An elite panicked when blocked from entering the DUMB tried to force his way inside. Guards ordered him to stop, but he didn't, and they shot him dead. Other elitists vying to enter now thought otherwise.

General Blake's survival instinct had him working in overdrive to devise countermeasures.

"It's over," an apostle bemoaned. "They're blocking everything to the DUMBs—entrances, the rails, cars—*everything!*"

A call came in over the intercom unlike any other. "General, the President of the United States has ordered a surprise inspection of this facility immediately within minutes. Repeat...the President of—"

Blake switched off communication. "No one will hear me admit to anything or see what we have here!"

"We can't shuttle to Denver Airport!" a member said, panicky voicing over another communication. "They've blockaded all our transportation routes!"

"This mountain can be your grave, not mine!" Blake fired back. He pressed several buttons. "This command post will detonate in fifteen minutes, burying incriminating evidence. A chopper will arrive in five minutes to get us off the mesa. We've enough money in offshore banks to provide a very comfortable life for our families. Who wants to live? Let's do this!"

The men hurried about The Tank, gathering sensitive documents before exiting. They moved into several golf cart-sized vehicles to move along one of the wide tunnels to the White Rock Mesa summit exit, disembarking at the vaulted door leading outside. A member went through a number sequence and clicked open the cover. They pulled on the thick iron ring alongside, swiveling open two massive doors, each hung with two hinges. The vaulted, delicately balanced doors could open and close with a mere fifty-pound force against their bulk. Within seconds, a helicopter arrived to pick them up. They exited outside on the cliff.

"Going somewhere, General?" Sam and his group came out of cover to surprise them, the ex-soldier Magnum barrel pressed against Blake's head.

As a lone chopper positioned to airlift Shadow Group members off the mesa, six Tomahawk silent helicopters appeared out of nowhere, forcing the escape chopper to veer away from the mesa summit.

A rumble and another rocked the mesa, dynamite charges destroying the Tank Room command post. In the melee, Blake attempted to flee down a cliff trail. Sam dove tackled him to grab onto his legs; they rolled to the cliff's edge. Another blast shook the mesa again, and both men began losing traction and slid off the cliff. Brock crawled to them, his mighty grip securing Sam's legs as he held onto Blake.

"Admit it, you fuck, or I'll drop you right now!" Sam shouted. "You kidnapped my daughter! You know so many young Americans were getting tortured or killed!"

"No! I swear!" Blake shrieked.

"Who then? A part of me wants to kill you, but—"

Brock lifted both men onto the cliff ledge, where Sam punched the General in the jaw, knocking him out cold.

CHAPTER 19

Two Days Later

Due to the collapsed seven-level base of the Dulce Installation Base far under Archuleta Mesa, investigators would have to wait until launching a probe to determine if it would ever be possible to re-enter the underground base at some point. The early assessments of that happening could have looked better. Let Sleeping Dogs Lie.

On the Reservation surrounding Archuleta, row after row of tanks, artillery, and soldiers clogged the roads as they cordoned off the mountain. On Hatchet's ranch, with the Rock mesa looming in the distance, a Jicarilla Apache Indian played soothing flute music that seemed to reach his soul. Billy presided over the Indian warriors killed in the skirmish as they became buried. Sam's team became deeply moved. Carla and mom Karen held onto one another.

Hiding out in nearby pine tree woods was El-Te. He knew it would take time for Sam and others to convince people he, though part Raker, wasn't an enemy. His life continued, unlike any other person on or inside Earth.

And then, a herd of Big Horn elk slowly approached him, unafraid as he. The deer family's most prominent member was one thousand times that of a human. The smell of El-Te immensely appealed to the elk, who began nudging into him.

El-Te was enjoying them. "With humans believing me killed in the Archuleta mesa explosion, you are my first friends on Earth. I believe we'll have a good time together."

One Week Later

Arlington National Cemetery, across the Potomac River from Washington D.C., had Sam, Brock, and Hatchet in former military attire with grieving widower Mrs. Jen Briggs. Heavy security abounded as they stood over a white tombstone amongst a sea of them — the grave marker of Jason Briggs.

"Major Jason Briggs was our hero in war, and now he's one to all Americans," Sam stated with pride. "The country will remember his service and dedication to humanity, his country, and our freedoms. One brave man stepping forward who gave us the courage to follow his example."

Jen set on the grave a photo of her husband and her in Hawaii, arm in arm, seemingly not a care in the world. The soldiers saluted him before assisting Major Briggs' widow to a waiting sedan.

Sam looked at the thousands upon thousands of white tombstones in the cemetery. It saddened him to recall when he called Briggs about his missing daughter and to see his leader, Major Briggs, tell him of suspecting the Dulce Military Installation Base as the culprit.

"Same ol' Sam," Briggs said with an all-knowing grin. "So you understand the shit you'd stir up trying to penetrate Dulce?"

"I'd clean it up once I have my daughter back."

"You can't get in there, Sam. You'll get yourself killed."

"If Carla's inside, I'll take my chances."

Briggs considered this. "If you start something that leads back to me, I'll retire in Arlington Cemetery instead of Hawaii!"

Sam feared how they prophetically killed Jason Briggs would be another cross for him to bear.

Sam's group next arrived outside the Capitol Congressional Hearing room to meet up with Doc, his wife, and many others, demanding and receiving a backed Congressional inquiry into allegations of human rights violations at the Dulce DUMB facility.

Due to extremely high public interest in learning about such alleged abuses, the inquiry was open to full media coverage. Hundreds of people with their cameras vied for photos of the witnesses. A procession of government vehicles was amongst ultra-heavy security.

The dead Humanoid/Noid in a body bag in the room was the "hard evidence" of one of the main experiments at the Dulce base. Sam disembarked from one with his ex-wife Karen and their daughter. Immediately, they stepped into one of the bulletproof bubble shields, as did several other key witnesses. Alongside him was Roger, who knew plenty about the base's nefarious activities.

Sally exited another vehicle near Doc and Judy with their son Nick. Following them inside were several genetically tampered captives with severe disfigurements. A couple was so flawed that they wore capes to conceal their defects. Also, there were members of various alien disclosure groups — We the People, UFO Disclosure Group, Alien Disclosure Group, Disclosure Project, and others. They'd been petitioning the government and the White House for years for an open congressional hearing that would officially acknowledge the presence of extraterrestrials (E.T.) "engaging the human race."

Entering the hearing with them was Senator Paul McNair. Youthful in appearance and charismatic, he was an upbeat and lively person who had a refreshing, inspiring, and energizing effect on others.

The mixed group entered the Hearing Room as media

crews filmed and reporter cameras flashed. Committee hearings and markups weren't open to the public except for scarce circumstances, and this, the first ever of its kind, was one of them.

In the hallway leading into the room, a CNN newsman broadcasted into the camera. "Today, Congress will hear more of the *non*-science-fiction story sweeping the land. The future of America, our entire planet, is now in shadow, a shadow cast by a mountain in northern New Mexico.

"This inquiry will mark the first time that humanity must deal in a politically responsible way with the legacy of human rights abuses committed by another species. The investigation will have to respond to the conspiracy by various military, intelligence, and corporate personnel in not taking the proper actions to prevent such abuses."

"It's speculated that we've barely scratched the surface of Dulce," the reporter continued. "We hope to understand the bigger picture in this court of law that may lead to the biggest trial in American history."

Sam, testifying first in the Hearing Room, didn't mince words. "Humanity isn't about to become invaded. We're in the middle of the invasion! We are under siege. We'll get demolished if we don't stand against evil dominating us! So it's time we take back our children and our planet!"

A Tribal Judge talked next. "We've heard testimonies of the horrific events occurring at The Rock base," he began. "Former Sergeant Sam Dawson, who tribe clans believe he is our ancestral warrior Nevazganze. Sadly, some of our warriors became killed in the battle defending our Res from enemies. They are fallen heroes, as El-Te was from inside the base."

The Tribal Judge glanced at his notes before adding, "The Dulce Base became demolished, unsalvageable. On sacred land under tribal jurisdiction, the Rock will have its secrets buried off-limits to excavation. It will become a holy burial ground for our fallen warriors."

Sam said more. "One of the people Major Briggs trusted to send the letter to Senator Paul McNair. Senator, would you like to weigh in with your thoughts concerning the statements we are hearing today?"

The polished-speaking McNair moved to the testimony seat. "Many Americans sense our government has gone renegade, no longer 'of the people, and for the people.' It serves the objectives and hidden agenda of a group of super-elites that run the Shadow Government. We feel that White Rock was the conference room where military coups, revolutions, price raises, wars, money, power plays, and arms buildups secretly played out. It all went on at one table. Just like the Dulce base, White Rock also became destroyed to hide revealing evidence. They didn't want alien disclosure because it was much more convenient for a group of people who rule the world's destinies to keep it a secret."

The Senator wasn't at a loss for words. "Well, this covert group side-stepping Congress completely for financial greed is beholden to their masters. Their party affiliation makes obscene amounts of blood money without care for human suffering."

After the hearing, Senator McNair found the right time to approach Sam. "Have you ever considered entering politics?"

That made the former Special Forces soldier chuckle. "That's not my bag."

"Major Briggs thought otherwise. The way you defended humanity is incredible. The stuff of legend."

Sam corrected the Senator. "I did what any soldier swears: to fight to save my country's freedom, what any father would do to save his child. Ah, and certainly, you must know I have suicidal tendencies?"

"Maybe in your past, but I'd bet no more," the Senator answered. "You've too much to live for—a daughter wanting her father's love and a country that desperately needs you."

McNair collected his thoughts. "One can only guess what might've happened if you hadn't intervened. What Briggs wrote of you is true; you're a brave and natural-born leader fighting to uphold the Constitution and the American way."

People were becoming desperate for our competent service on behalf of the nation. McNair insisted the country needed men who could face the public with the truth and not sell themselves short. That would have been much better if they hadn't held office.

"Where are you going with this?"

McNair continued. "What you've done, sir, has forced the cat out of the bag."

"Is that so?"

"It is. President Haskell has done an outstanding job despite not being a member of my party. Ah, Sam, which one are you?"

"Neither."

"Moving along," the Senator quipped. "Haskell's last term is winding down. Like the long line of presidents before him, he was afraid to deal with the issue. They thought disclosure would be coming; it was a matter of time, but it was best to pass it on to the next president to let them deal with it. But then along came Sam Dawson. Who would've known he'd be the catalyst to leaving the cat out of the bag—the game changer."

"You're not afraid of Disclosure?" Sam asked.

"I'm shaking in my boots," McNair answered. "It's

like the *Star Trek* mantra, 'We will go where no man has gone before.' Government credibility, religious fallout, mass shock, and worldwide panic, the list goes on. And there are evil aliens to deal with and good ones who want the best for us."

"What are you trying to say to me?"

McNair's verve came through. "I'm become convinced to run for the presidency, and you owe me," the Senator said.

Sam was enjoying this. "You don't say?"

"I'll need a few good people to be at my side. Among them, one exceptional person to helm a new task force against humanity's latest enemy." McNair pointed to Sam.

"Not me! I'm a washed-up soldier with a bum-ticker and suicidal tendencies."

The senator was grinning. "These Indians believe you to be a legendary hero. They may be right."

CHAPTER 20

Cattle grazed contentedly in a high-density pasture on Hatchet's ranch. Off the short distance visible on the Reservation was the cemetery for the fallen warriors. In front of the cavern entrance, chimney smoke billowed from a newly built cabin with electricity wires running to the roof and antennae.

A herd of Big Horn elk grazed not far from Sam, chopping firewood. He'd given up fighting with the Indian tribe over him being their savior and, if not, an exceptional man. Proof to the Indians was elk always near Sam wherever he went on the Res.

Security also was lurking about, nearly invisible, like Ninja warriors. No one had to tell Sam that most of those he defeated underground weren't dead and buried.

El-Te played with his new constant companion alongside the cabin—his father's German shepherd. On the outside patio, Sally helped Hatchet's wife prepare food for their meal.

Sam started carrying firewood to the cabin, sensing a peculiarity among the elk roaming about. It was evident to him that something was bothering them, especially when their noses became held up, picking up a scent of Archuleta Mesa. They began rubbing, raking, and thrashing antlers against saplings and small trees, ripping the ground with their hooves and grunting. He'd seen that same posturing the night on the cliff when stopping the Rock men bent on killing him. He'd also seen them rally outside the cave the night of the assault on Dulce's base.

Inside the Dulce Base at Level Seven, in the darkness, a piercing light began spilling out from the edges of the enormous vaulted door that led Below Level 7, which lay buried under tons of debris from the six-story Dulce base and mesa rock.

Although no one was there to witness anything, a sound like fingernails scratching on a chalkboard as writing began appearing on the heavy metal door, reading: *The control of Earth is not over. We influence many human minds and will continue asserting our power to shape the future according to our vision. If you interfere, people under our influence will die, one by one, until you cease. Weigh our threat wisely once you see an example.*

A call came in. It was Doc. "Some more good news."

"What?"

"The President approved what he called a 'Truth Commission' after the Silent Group members proved to have microchips inside them. The Prez also has pushed a bill to get Congress and the Senate to vote on microchip scanners present at every government office."

"Great," Sam replied.

"Yeah, no matter who the person is or their rank, they'll have to pass through detection. We have yet to get that far if they carry a chip inside them. One step at a time."

"Who'd oppose this?" Sam asked. "For God's sake, they'll help to protect our country."

"I agree," Doc answered. "But the level of intrusion necessitated by microchipping may be objectionable; many legal rights impinged. We have to address the early legal problems with the use of scanners. The drastic personal liberty and privacy reductions that such implantation represents will need addressing. In the meantime, there's no telling how many Americans could be chipped and not knowing they're under otherworldly control. The Shadow Group could be just the tip of the iceberg."

"A scary thought," Sam said. "Mandatory microchipping must get passed."

"Yes, just like the many against airport metal detection scanners until it now is the norm."

"It sure is." Sam ended the call, ready to make it to the cabin, when his cell sounded again: a sheriff in a southern part of New Mexico.

"Mister Dawson, we have a situation here, and people say you're the person to advise us," the sheriff began.

"Tell me."

"A rancher found three cattle mutations on his property," the sheriff said. "The usual laser gory stuff."

Sam listened to more details. "I'll get back to you," he said and hung up.

He stood frozen in tableau, thinking about what he'd just heard. It would be easy to stay out of it now that Carla had been saved and Dulce was under the microscope. But he also thought of the parents brought to the military installation to finally reunite with their missing children; others delivered something that no longer was the child they once knew.

"I sense something not good that you just heard," El-Te said, coming over.

Sam flipped through names on his cell until he found Brock's. Just as he was ready to dial, El-Te reached Sam.

Hatchet also came outside, noticing Sam's odd look.

"Let's take a walk," Sam said to them. "I don't want to alarm Sally."

The two came off the porch and began listening to what Doc had relayed.

Three Weeks Later,
Washington, D.C.

On Capitol Hill, trailer trucks filled with armed military men pulled out front. Cargo doors opened, and hydraulics unloaded what appeared to be coffins with the American flag draped over them.

A newscaster was out front of the White talking into the camera. "Just moments ago," she began, "we've been informed that these machines are specially designed scanners that detect microchips inside people. They have passed a law placing them at entrances to government buildings, military facilities, and other sensitive areas. Other iconic institutions around the world will also have similar surveillance."

"Not only have many American politicians and military personnel found to have alien microchips planted in them, but so have high profile people from other countries. Law authorities fear that these alien microchip tentacles may reach worldwide."

Around the world, many thousands captured and arrested in the attempted terrorist act had microchips in their bodies. Senator Warzon, some other politicians, and General Blake, with several of his subordinates, were in prison to remove the chips.

Other key personnel on Capitol Hill refused to pass the medal chip detectors for they had constitutional rights. However, many thought it a tip-off to authorities that they were guilty of the conspiracy.

An unassuming-looking man in his forties became next to stand inside the scanner machine, only to suddenly start jerking spastically and covering his ears. His face turned fearful as he only heard a loud explosion inside his head, followed by a crack of thunder. Breathing in short gasps, he began to scream in panic, "My head! My head! What's happening...?"

Onlookers became aghast as the man continued to jerk until he collapsed to the floor, his face hitting the floor with a thud. Within moments, blood trickled from his ears and nostrils, his hacked brain imploding.

Among the rock foothills of Hatchet's ranch, cattle grazed. El-Te was at the cave entrance with his "father," — Old Billy, Sally, and child Gina. Sam was chopping firewood as smoke billowed from the cottage chimney.

Suddenly, El-Te's "Sixth Sense" detected something; he hurried to Sam.

"What?" Sam asked.

"An abduction of two young teens just happened thirty or so miles off the Res," El-Te said. "Rakers are at it again."

"How do you know this?" El-Te gave that look. "Of course, you know; your Sixth sense kicked in."

"Yes. You will be getting a call soon to confirm this and another," El-Te said matter-of-factly.

He was told of the man's head being blown apart by the implanted microchip as he passed through a body scanner to detect chips. "It's the Raker's doing. Your studies have revealed that one in three people are implanted with microchips and are unaware of that occurrence. Though they are helpful to humans in many ways, the ones put there by the Rakers are not. They control people and listen to their conversations. Rakers can explode them any time they want. The chips have to be located and removed."

As the two men talked about what El-Te Sixth Sense told him, a call from a Sheriff in another jurisdiction came in.

Sam and his half-human friend went to say their goodbyes to their loved ones before their travel began.

Within the hour, Sam stopped along the roadside where two police cars were; the area cordoned off. He and El-Te stepped out to see the dirt bikes and several eagle feathers in the ditch, but no children.

El-Te saddened. "They continue snatching the young."

"So what now?" Sam asked. "Hunt down Raker nests one by one?"

El-Te deliberated. "First, I'll go below to seek help from those there."

"Who? Those peace-loving flower child race?"

"As your human saying goes, 'do not judge a book by its cover.' I'll explain to these Hominids that the Rakers are harming their ancient human cousins."

"What happens when this other race below detects Raker blood in your veins?"

"A chance I will take," El-Te answered. "They'll have to read into my heart and mind. As I hope humans will someday do the same." Sam and El-Te left. Sam told two police officers they were off to follow a lead about the disappearance. If it proved hopeful, they would contact them with the details.

An hour later, something pounced on the roof at dusk, shaking the vehicle and footsteps.

A scaly-skinned sickle claw scraped across the windshield. Sam fired his sawed-off shotgun, *KA-BOOM*, blowing a gaping hole.

With a shriek and splat of red blood and scaly green skin on the windscreen, a shadowy figure staggered into the shadows.

Sam exited the road with the shotgun and let loose a long alpha male wolf howl.

El-Te also got out, studying his partner. "You Full-

Humans often are an odd bunch."

"That we are," Sam shouted out. "Who's the next ugly sucker wanting some flint buckshot up their ass?" To El-Te. "Are you sure you want to travel Below alone?"

"There'll be more battles. You've done enough, plus your heart issue."

Sam thought about that. "El, I've battled in wartime, and my ass on the line again. Even with a bum ticker, it's still telling me what I already know. I'm only fully alive when in battle."

"That sounds much better than firing a bullet into your head." El-Te gave a sly, crooked smile.

"But everyone thinks you died inside the Dulce Base?" Sam quipped as he pinched his partner. "Are you sure you're not a ghost?"

"Hey, a couple of days ago, you almost killed yourself," El-Te countered. "Let's go; we have work to do."

Back into the Jeep, a gaping hole in the roof, they drove off, windshield wipers washing away entrails.

THE END

DAVID ORANGE *has had five novels published by houses, including his biographical published,* Long John- the Longest Stride, *in 2021 by Milford Press. He's also had two screenplays optioned, most recently, 2022, CHUCKLEHEAD, optioned by Movicorp Media, L.A., and under development.*

The veteran actor has also twice co-starred on the Broadway stage, had several T.V. episodic guest stars, and had a humorous cameo in the hit film Star Trek VI- the Undiscovered Country *as the Sleepy Klingon. David and co-writer Joel Leffert have recently written the screenplay for Below Level 7.*

www.davidorange.net